Faro's Wild West—
Where Cleanliness
Is Next to Impossible!

Faro heard a voice from the other side of the bath-house. "I knew if you stayed here long enough we would meet eventually, but I had no idea it would be under such revealing circumstances."

Faro turned around, startled at the sound of a woman's voice, and saw the major's wife, Marantha Volney, standing near the door. With no visible signs of embarrassment, the woman was looking him over carefully from head to foot, seeming to take his measure both as a whole, and by his separate parts. And by the appreciative grin which soon crossed her features, he seemed to measure up in her estimation. . . .

Books by Zeke Masters

Published by POCKET BOOKS

#15

A ZEKE MASTERS WESTERN

PLACE YOUR BETS

PUBLISHED BY POCKET BOOKS NEW YORK

Another *Original* publication of POCKET BOOKS

POCKET BOOKS, a Simon & Schuster division of
GULF & WESTERN CORPORATION
1230 Avenue of the Americas, New York, N.Y. 10020

ISBN: 0-671-43814-X

First Pocket Books printing April, 1982

10 9 8 7 6 5 4 3 2 1

POCKET and colophon are trademarks of Simon & Schuster.

Printed in the U.S.A.

PLACE YOUR
BETS

Chapter One

The forest floor the two men were riding over seldom felt the warmth of sunlight, and above their heads the sky was only occasionally visible through the thick upper branches of the towering redwood trees. A cathedrallike atmosphere existed here in this patch of north California woodland. The air was still about them, and hardly any birds or other small woodland creatures seemed to inhabit this grove of spectacular earthbound giants.

Confronted by the overwhelming spectacle of the lofty redwoods which surrounded them, Faro Blake was moved to comment with reverent awe, "Big fuckers, ain't they?"

Few of the redwoods around them had branches any closer than one hundred feet to the ground, and some of the larger ones were as much as twenty feet in diameter and three hundred feet tall.

"Big trees, big profits, Mr. Blake," his companion,

Hobart Nye, commented smugly. Ever since they had left the expanses of more ordinary forest to the south and entered the homeland of these titans, Nye had been in a tizzy of excitement. "I control the logging rights to nearly a thousand acres in this area, and with an average of forty trees per acre, and two hundred thousand board feet of lumber per tree . . ."

In his mind, Faro could picture the little egg-shaped man slouched over a desk in some dingy, dimly lit hotel room, filling page after page with calculations of the million-dollar profits he dreamed of making in this enterprise. But they were abstract and practically meaningless numbers to Faro; the largest sums he usually chose to consider were the healthy amounts shoved into a poker pot during a high-stakes game.

"By my estimates," Nye continued, "it would take nearly thirty thousand dollars just to begin operations here, but within three months, when the first wagonloads of lumber start rolling south toward Sacramento and San Francisco, the profits would start flowing in almost faster than we could count them. Why, within a year, Mr. Blake . . ."

What seemed to repeatedly come to mind when Faro looked at Nye was a drawing of Humpty-Dumpty which he remembered from a childhood book of rhymes. His squat body was shaped in a perfect wide oval, with skinny little stick legs and arms which seemed to have been added as an afterthought and a balding, fleshy round head. The features of his face were constantly arranged into a wide, solicitous smile, and even here in the remote forest he was dressed like a sideshow spieler in a green- and white-striped suit and a round bowler hat.

But, if he was small, Nye had a cocky, arrogant confidence and a glib line which did not match his diminutive size. He thought big and he talked big, and now Faro felt obliged to at least listen to his sales pitch after accepting so many drinks and dinners at Nye's expense over the past few days.

"Can't you just picture it in your mind?" Nye continued. "Hundreds of workmen lopping these big sons of bitches off at the ground and sawing them into timber to build homes and businesses all the way from Los Angeles to Portland. Imagine mountains of timber being stacked up, waiting for shipment to the coastal markets, while our profits multiply and pile up in our San Francisco bank accounts. And all that could be yours, Mr. Blake, for a very reasonable sum, a mere pittance of an investment considering the returns . . ."

Faro had over five thousand dollars on him, more than enough to buy a sizable percentage of Nye's operation, but he had no intention of doing that. The only kind of gambling he cared anything about was the kind done facing another man across a gaming table, and his true reasons for being here had nothing whatsoever to do with redwood trees, mountains of lumber, or buildings in San Francisco. Simply put, this time spent with Nye was just a minor diversion during a journey from someplace that he didn't want to be to someplace that he did.

The place that he didn't want to be just now was San Francisco. Past experience had told him that lead in the air made for a seriously unhealthy climate, especially when some of that lead was shaped into bullets and propelled out of the end of a gun in his direction.

The curious sequence of events which had led him here to the land of the giant trees had begun a few weeks ago in the back parlor of a Chinese whorehouse in San Francisco. He had gone there for the customary reasons after a casual acquaintance in a hotel bar had described to him the incredible experiences to be had in the arms of a certain slant-eyed beauty named Som Chew. His interlude with the petite, talented Chinese girl had been well worth the twenty-dollar price he had paid, but later, as he was preparing to leave, he had been drawn to the rear of the house by the unmistakable epithets of a crap game.

Normally craps was low on Faro's list of ways to make money at his chosen profession of gambling. The percentages were too low, and no amount of skill or practice could give a professional an appreciable edge over an amateur. Besides that, the ways to cheat were numerous and sometimes quite difficult to detect. But on that particular night Faro was not at work and had decided to risk a few dollars simply for the fun of it. The evening, however, provided a perfect case in point to show how things never worked out quite like a man thought they would.

When he left the whorehouse a few hours later, his pockets were bulging with several hundred dollars, mostly in small gold coins and low-denomination paper money, that he had won in the game, and in the inside front pocket of his suit jacket was the deed to, of all things, a gold mine. He had won the mine from an incoherent drunken fool to whom regaining the pittance he had lost in the crap game seemed more important than hanging on to what could provide a lifetime of wealth and security.

Normally Faro would not have accepted such a deed in lieu of a hard-cash bet, but he remembered reading in the San Francisco newspapers some weeks back about the opening of this particular mine, the Estrella del Norte. Soon after its discovery, some of the first ore had assayed out at nearly a thousand dollars per ton, and the initial investment for equipment and supplies had been recouped during the first month of operation.

Later, in his hotel room, he spent a sleepless night filled with fantasies about the places he would see, the luxuries he would wallow in, and the splendid women which his newly acquired wealth would draw to him. He rose at dawn the next morning, rented a horse, and began the two-day ride to the remote gold fields to inspect his new acquisition, expecting to find a mountainside teeming with busy miners and carts loaded with glittering ore pouring out of the Estrella del Norte.

Things were not quite that way when he arrived. The village of shacks which had housed the scores of mine workers was now a ghost town, the ore carts sat empty on their narrow-gauge rails, and the gaping entrance to the mine itself penetrated only about a hundred yards into the mountainside. After wandering the area in a daze for a while, Faro finally ended up at the frame building which had apparently served as the mine office. Engineering reports which he found scattered out on the floor there filled in the details of the sad demise of the Estrella del Norte. The vein of gold-bearing quartz which looked so promising at first had played out completely when it reached a thick vertical barrier of granite. The shelf of valuable ore might continue at some point on the opposite side of the granite, or it might not. Geographic upheavals might have shifted the vein hundreds of feet higher or lower, or to either side. The report indicated that an investment of as much as fifty thousand dollars might be necessary to continue further exploration, and then the chances for success were still rated no better than one in twenty.

Sherman Perkins, the man Faro had won the mine from, had apparently kept the week-old report a secret, because no news of the closing of the Estrella del Norte had appeared in the San Francisco newspapers. Maybe,

Faro realized suddenly, Perkins had not been as doltish as he looked or as mindlessly drunk as he had acted. At any rate, he was clever enough to fool Faro Blake, a man who prided himself on knowing most of the scams there were to pull and seeing through most of the deceits anybody tried to work on him.

As soon as the initial wave of disappointment and anger passed, though, Faro's thoughts began to run in a different direction. If he really put his mind to it, there must be a way to turn a profit even from a situation as ridiculous as this one. All during the ride back he brooded about it, and by the time he reached San Francisco two days later, a plan had taken shape in his mind.

The first thing next morning he went to a local printer and bought a package of the most expensive writing paper in stock. Then he spent the rest of the morning in his hotel room thoroughly studying the five-page engineering report on the Estrella del Norte mine, which he had thought to bring along with him. It had been compiled by the firm of Edmunson and Mc-Gruder, one of the most prestigious mining-engineering firms on the West Coast. The first page of the report bore the firm's embossed letterhead, but the remaining four pages were on regular paper similar to that which Faro had bought that morning.

For hours he practiced with pen and paper, attempting to duplicate the handwriting of whoever had written out the original report. When he decided he had that reasonably well mastered, he painstakingly recopied the last four pages of the report, making only a few strategic changes which altered the entire findings of the report. In the now-revised opinion of Edmunson and McGruder, the Estrella del Norte was no longer a lost cause but could most likely be saved with the

investment of about five thousand dollars for special-
ized equipment to penetrate the granite barrier.

By eight that evening the five revised pages of the
report were spread out on the table before him, and
Faro leaned back in his chair to stretch some of the
stiffness out of his neck and shoulders.

"Not bad," he commented to himself with a wide
grin of satisfaction. "Nosiree, not bad a-tall. Old Doc
would be proud of me if he could see this day's work."
The Doc he was referring to was Jackson Lafitte "Doc"
Prentiss—also known as Andy Jackson, Colonel
Humphrey Rowayton, Reverend Jonas Pott, Chief
Spotted Tail, and only the devil knew what else—who
was a longtime friend and mentor of Faro's, as well as
the best damn con man ever to bilk a willing sucker
out of his life's savings or the small change in his
pocket. Though Faro had not chosen to follow in Doc
Prentiss's footsteps on a full-time basis, he did on
occasion find use for some of the tricks of the con
man's trade which Doc had drilled into his head as a
youth.

Now, with the report copied, Faro was ready to put
the second part of his plan into operation. He had to
find a mark somewhere who would be willing to take
the Estrella del Norte off his hands on the basis of the
mine's past production and the optimistic findings in
the altered document. That part, he thought, would be
as difficult as recopying the report had been, but at
least it would be a little more entertaining.

He waited until later in the evening, past ten o'clock,
to head out on his search. By that time of night more
men had their brains fogged by alcohol and were more
willing to believe tall tales and take gambles that they
would not in their more sober moments. He crossed
several blocks of the city until he reached the part of
town where most of the exclusive men's clubs and more

elite saloons were located. The first law of a gambler's life was that if he wanted to make money he had to go where the money was. Somewhere in the Nob Hill district of San Francisco, where the moneyed class of the city led their lives of garish splendor and snobbery, he knew he would find precisely the man he was seeking.

After stopping briefly in three or four other establishments, he finally chose to make his play in the glittering Pacific Palace Emporium. The Pacific Palace was a combination restaurant, saloon, casino, and brothel. The place featured some of the finest food and drink west of Denver, around-the-clock stage entertainment, scores of lovely hostesses who were available for conversation, copulation, and everything in between, and some of the fastest and most expensive gambling action on the West Coast.

Faro knew that one or two high-stakes poker games were probably going on behind some of the closed doors on the far side of the Pacific Palace, but that wasn't the kind of action he was looking for tonight. Instead he opted to take a seat at one of the more casual games in the main open area of the saloon. When the first cards in the five-man game of stud poker came sliding across the table to him, he had already decided on his role for the evening. He was the drunk and despondent owner of a mine near San Francisco who had come to the city with his last few hundred dollars in his pocket, desperate to win enough money to buy the equipment it would take to make his holdings profitable again. He played with an intentional lack of skill, but he made the five hundred dollars which he planned to lose last long enough for him to make a careful study of the other players around him. The man to his left was obviously outclassed in a place like this. He played his hands tight, folding too soon and betting too little, and he was losing as a result.

Faro quickly eliminated him as a possibility. The two men immediately to Faro's right seemed to be wealthy enough for his purposes, but since they were ranchers down from Wyoming on a spree, he thought it might be difficult to talk them into buying into a local mine if they could not be around to watch over their investment.

The big, blustering drunken fellow across the table from Faro seemed to be the most likely prospect. His meaty, battered, fifty-year-old features indicated that he was cut from a rough bolt of goods, but the expensive suit he wore and the solicitous attitude of the staff of the Pacific Palace spoke of wealth and heavy-handed influence. All during the game an endless stream of girls passed the table near him, gladly submitting to a pinch, pat, or fondle from the big man in exchange for a gold coin. Waiters hovered about him like flies, never letting him see the empty bottom of the large brandy glass he was drinking from. During the course of the game, Faro learned that the big man's name was Amos Harbison, but the chippies and waiters who knew him best referred to him simply as Knuckles.

In the card game, the man bet heavily on good hands and bad alike, buying some pots with the tactic but showing little concern when he lost big on others. For a while Faro considered abandoning the gold-mine business and making a grab for some of this man's money with straight-on, hard-nosed poker playing, but finally he decided against it. For one thing, he had already intentionally lost most of the cash he could have used for a stake in the game; and for another, he had no guarantee that the man would stay in the game long enough to lose nearly as much as Faro hoped to earn from the sale of the mine.

After about two hours of play, the moment which Faro had been waiting for finally came. The first four cards of the hand had been dealt, one down and three up, and Faro had the bid with two aces and a king showing. As he raised the corner of his hole card and glanced at the second king there, he thought, Daddy would sit up in his grave and disown me if he saw what I was about to do with a hand like this. He glanced around the table at the other players, letting a tight, nervous smile play across his lips, then wiped his forehead with his hand and cleared his throat. "Aces bet fifty," he said, shoving half of his remaining chips into the pot.

As the bet marched around the table three of the other players folded, leaving only Faro and the man called Knuckles still in. Faro's opponent had an ace, two, and five of hearts showing, indicating the possibility of a flush or even a straight flush. He matched Faro's bet, then raised it fifty dollars more. By the time Faro called the bet, he was broke.

The last card came sliding face down across the table from the Wyoming cattleman who was dealing, and Faro tipped the corner up only far enough to see that it was an ace. Faro glanced over at his opponent across the table, doing his best to look like a nervous man trying to show no expression whatsoever on his face. Knuckles was grinning like an alley cat in a fish market.

"Aces check," Faro said finally. It was the desperate ploy of an amateur who was hoping against hope that his opponent would check, too, and consent to play for the existing pot.

"Broke, huh?" The big man chuckled.

"That's right," Faro told him tensely.

"Well, that's some tough shit, mister," Knuckles told him, reaching inside his jacket for his wallet. He pulled out a stack of bills and announced with glee, "It'll cost you one thousand big ones to see what I got."

Faro just sat staring at his cards for a while, but finally, when his opponent reached out to gather in the pot, he said quickly, "Wait! I've got something else for collateral here if you'll accept it." He produced the deed and handed it across the table.

The big man took the deed and opened it up, but he was so drunk that he seemed to have difficulty making his eyes focus on the words. "What the fuck is it?" he mumbled at last.

"It's the deed to a gold mine," Faro told him. "The Estrella del Norte. If you'll agree, I'll offer you, say, one-fourth interest in the mine if I lose this hand. If you win, your share could be worth ten times the thousand dollars you've laid out pretty soon."

"Shee-it!" the big man grumbled, pitching the deed back at Faro. "Paper like that floats around this town all the time, and most of it ain't worth nothing." Then he got a sly grin on his face and added, "But I will let you bet the whole thing if you think your hand's that good. That's my deal. All the mine or nothing!"

Faro picked up the deed and acted as if he were agonizing over the decision for a moment. At one point he held it out as if to drop it into the pot, then drew it back suddenly and returned it to his pocket. "I can't," he exclaimed in defeat. "You take the damn pot."

As Knuckles began to rake in the hundreds of dollars between them he guffawed and said, "Ain't many times a man can turn a pile of shit like I got into a winning hand!" He flipped his two down cards over and showed that neither of them fit in with the straight flush that he might have had. "I'd say, mister," he went on, "that either you're mighty long on caution or else you really do have yourself a gold mine that's worth hangin' on to."

"Most times I'm not such a careful man," Faro admitted. "But I know what I've got even if nobody else does, and I'd be a blamed fool to risk it on the turn of a card . . . even with a hand like this." He turned over his two hole cards, revealing the aces-over-kings full house he held.

Faro rose from the table and turned as if to start away, but instead he looked back at Knuckles and said, "Since you're the one that busted me, how about buying me a drink? I hadn't got enough cash left to even pay for a shot of whiskey."

"Hell, yes, I'll buy you a drink," Knuckles announced heartily. "Let's haul it over to the bar and I'll buy you all the damn drinks you can slug back."

Faro followed his companion's wobbly lead across the crowded room, and when they reached the long mahogany bar, Knuckles hollered for the attention of one of the half-dozen bartenders on duty. "The usual for me, Tim," Knuckles told the bartender, "and for my friend here . . . what're you drinking?"

"Bourbon," Faro said.

". . . and bourbon for my friend, Tim."

"The name's Simon Carmody," Faro told him.

When their drinks arrived, Knuckles took a healthy swallow of his, then told Faro, "I'd say, Carmody, that you chose the wrong way to pick up a little extra cash for yourself. You ain't worth a shit at playing poker."

"I know," Faro told him worriedly. "It's just that I'm getting desperate for some operating capital. I know this mine I own could come in big, but . . . well, here. Let me show you something."

From an inside pocket he drew out the altered engineering report and handed it to Knuckles.

"Whassis?" Knuckles asked in confusion.

"It's a report on the survey that Edmunson and Mc-Gruder did on the Estrella del Norte," Faro told him. "The quartz vein we were following hit a granite fissure and stopped, but look here on page three. They say the vein likely picks up and widens out on the other side of the granite. They say the best way to get through is with a steam-powered drill that I could get for five thousand dollars in Denver.

"That's why I came here," he went on, "to try to turn my five hundred dollars into five thousand so I could buy that drill. But then I had the rotten luck to run up against a sharp player like you and lose every cent. It's just the way things've been going for me lately."

Knuckles was reading over the report as thoroughly as his fogged mind would permit, and it was obvious that he was interested. "So you ain't got the five thousand dollars it would take to get rich," he said finally, with a chuckle.

"Ain't it a bitch?" Faro said.

Knuckles gazed at him appraisingly, for a moment, then said, "I'll tell you the truth, Carmody. I ain't never dabbled in the mining business none. Railroads are my game. Twenty years ago I used to help build them, and now I own them. But I never been a man to let a good opportunity slip by me when I could help it. I'll give you the money for this drill you need in exchange for a share in the mine. How does fifty-fifty sound to you?"

"Fifty-fifty!" Faro exclaimed angrily. "You've got to be out of your damn mind if you think I'd grab a deal like that. Why, once I get past that granite, this mine's likely to earn fifty thousand dollars a month. Maybe more."

"It might," Knuckles told him cagily. "Or it might earn diddly-squat. But you won't know either way until you drill through that granite and find out, and right now it looks to me like you ain't making much progress toward finding out anything. Matter of fact, you're going backward. Five thousand dollars for half of the mine, Carmody. That's my offer."

Faro began to agonize again. He had been doing quite a bit of that tonight and thought he was getting pretty good at it. "I can see how you earned all the money you got, Harbison," Faro said at last. "You're a hard-nosed son of a bitch. All right, it's a deal."

Within half an hour Faro's companion had come up with five thousand dollars in hard cash and Faro had signed the name Simon Carmody to a receipt acknowledging the sale of half interest in the Estrella del Norte Mine. At the close of the transaction Faro had also grudgingly passed the deed over to Harbison for safekeeping. Their agreement was that Faro would go to Denver and purchase the steam drill, and then, when he got back, he would take over the deed again, as well as management of the mine.

Soon Faro returned to his hotel room, his pocket bulging with the fat bundle of bank notes, and smugly turned in for a night's sleep.

The next morning he took his time packing his things to leave. It should take days, he thought, before Knuckles Harbison discovered the swindle, and even then there would be very little that he could do against Faro in court. Legally, Faro had done nothing but make a legitimate sale of an actual mine. (He had thoughtfully brought the engineering report back with him to the hotel room, where he had carefully burned it before going to bed.) Still, though, Faro did not plan to be around when Harbison made the discovery. When the westbound afternoon stage left for Sacramento, he would be on it. The days of the big gold strikes out in that direction were long since past, but there was still plenty of good prospecting to be done in the saloons and casinos of Sacramento.

As Faro came down the stairs from the second floor of the hotel, carrying his valise in one hand and his case of advantage gambling tools in the other, he noticed some sort of commotion in the lobby below. He paused midway down the stairs and slipped his hand inside his dark suit coat to draw the small Reid's knuckleduster derringer which he always carried there. The stubby little weapon fit comfortably in the palm of his hand, with only the brass knuckles which were built onto the handle showing on the outside of his fingers. Then he started down again, this time alert for trouble.

The morning clerk who usually manned the front desk at this time of day was hung neatly by the back of his jacket onto a coat hook by the front door, his feet dangling a good twelve inches off the floor. His face showed that he was more than a little afraid as he stared helplessly at the two men across the lobby. One of them was behind the desk, carefully examining each entry in the registration book, while the other stood by, calmly honing a matchstick into a toothpick with the blade of a ten-inch knife.

Both were big, muscle-bound bruisers, the kind that could probably come up with several hundred ways to kill or maim a man but were never quite sure how their names were spelled. As he gazed at them Faro felt a funny little knot of tension grab his midsection.

"You sure you ain't never heard of this Carmody feller?" the man behind the desk asked the suspended morning clerk.

"Nuh-nuh-no, sir, I ain't," the clerk stuttered out. Either he was plenty scared, Faro observed, or else he had spilled a glass of water down the crotch of his britches not long before these fellows came calling.

"You're dead sure?" the man with the knife asked, waving his blade for emphasis. "Me 'n' Angus would

be damned upset if we found out later you was lyin'
to us."

"It's the truth, Muh-muh-mister Cobb. Nobody
named Carmody has stayed here any time re-re-re-
cently."

Finally the one with the blade, who was apparently
named Cobb, turned to Faro and said, "What about
you, fartface?"

"What about me?" Faro asked. He was not at all
eager to mix it up with these two, but he was not about
to let them bully him, either. That would be the quick-
est way in the world, he figured, to end up on the
empty hook beside the dangling clerk.

"What's your name, smartass?" Cobb demanded.

"It's in the book," Faro said. "Faro Blake. I checked
in here a week ago."

Cobb glanced over at the clerk, who nodded his
head to verify Faro's identity.

"You ever met a man named Simon Carmody,
Blake?" Cobb asked.

"I don't know anybody with that name," Faro said.
"Why? What do you want with him, anyway?"

"We don't want him," the man behind the desk,
Angus, said. "Our boss, Mr. Amos Harbison, wants
him. He sent us out this morning to find him and bring
him back."

"We didn't ask why," Cobb added. "We never do."

When the interrogations were finished and the two
were ready to leave, Cobb stopped by the door and
lifted the clerk down from the hook as easily as an
ordinary man would take a hat from a rack. But for a
moment he held the smaller man suspended in the air,
their two faces only inches apart, as he warned, "We
been checkin' all over town for this Carmody—in
hotels, the stage station, everywhere. And anybody that

sees him or even hears tell of him better get word to us pronto. I mean he *better!* You got that, little man?"

"He better," the clerk repeated dutifully.

"You got that shit straight, Blake?"

"Better," Faro said wearily. Taking just a little bit of shit was all right, he reasoned, if it meant seeing the last of these two.

When the two thugs were gone, the clerk scurried back around behind the desk for obvious and embarrassing reasons. Faro went over to the desk and set his valise and case on the floor, then said, "Total my tab up for me. I'm checking out this morning." Then, as the clerk was adding up the charges for his stay, he went on, trying to sound casual and only vaguely interested. "This Harbison fellow must really throw a lot of weight around San Francisco."

"Let's just say, if Knuckles Harbison's got it in for somebody called Simon Carmody, you better thank the lucky stars that ain't your name," the clerk said. "Harbison runs the rail yards of San Francisco like the czar runs Russia. In an hour he could dredge up enough muscle-headed railroad dicks like those two to give the whole San Francisco police force a good fight. But he don't really need to do that, 'cause he owns aplenty of the police and politicians in town, too."

Faro kept a poker face, not letting his reaction to that news show on his features. But inside he was berating himself for being every kind of dunderheaded fool in the book. He had been so cocky and confident about his scam that he had plunged straight into it without first taking a little time to check out his mark. And this situation was the payoff for his impatience.

After he paid his bill, Faro left the hotel and headed east toward the edge of the city instead of west where the stage station and railroad depot were located. If Harbison's men were watching those places, then taking a stage out of town today was definitely out. Along with the name, Harbison might well have gven his men a description of Simon Carmody, and that description was likely to fit the person of one Faro Blake entirely too well. He had been lucky back there in the hotel where he had had somebody to verify his identity, but someplace else he might not be so fortunate.

But one thing was sure. He did need to get the hell out of San Francisco, and the quicker he did that, the better his chances would be to avoid any inconvenient broken bones or discommodious holes in his body.

His rambling steps led him to the edge of town, where a wagon driver stopped unexpectedly and called down to him. "I'm headed north up toward Enterprise. If you need a ride, pitch your stuff in back and climb up on the seat." A sign on the side of the wagon announced that it was the property of Enterprise Logging and Lumber Co.

"It's bumpy, but it'll get us there," the driver assured him. "I'll be joining up with the company wagon train a few miles north of here, and from there it's a week's ride to Enterprise."

Suddenly the idea seemed very appealing to Faro. If Knuckles Harbison was looking all over San Francisco for him, then it made sense that he might also put a few feelers out in places like Sacramento and Los Angeles, too. It was not unthinkable that Harbison might actually be willing to spend more finding a man who had cheated him than he had lost in the original swindle.

The trip north with the logging-company wagon train was a peaceful and profitable one for Faro. Once the teamsters discovered his true profession, each night he was encouraged to haul out his faro layout for two or three hours of spirited betting, and day by day his bankroll gradually increased. When Faro first left San Francisco, he had it in mind to work his way as far north as Seattle or Vancouver, but now he was in no hurry to do it. All over the northern part of the state, he realized, there were hundreds of men who spent ninety-nine percent of their time in isolated logging camps and settlements, with very little entertainment to distract them from the incessant boredom. Every one of those men received a pay envelope each month, and most would be delighted to risk some or all of their wages on a game of chance. The bigger cities to the north would be there whenever he decided to visit them, but in the meantime there were plenty of profits to be skimmed from the men in the logging camps.

After parting from the wagon train in Enterprise, Faro bought a horse for himself and continued on north. He spent anywhere from a day to a week in several camps along the way, and eventually found himself in the town of Timberline, located in the north central part of the state.

Timberline had derived its name from its situation near the base of the eastern slopes of the Sierra Nevadas, close to where the heavy forests of the mountainside gave way to the lush valleys, lakes, and lava beds of the lowlands. The town thrived on the business from the logging camps to the north, south, and west, but it also served the needs of the many small ranches and farms located in the valleys to the east.

In the past two years, the U.S. Army had also established a fort about five miles east of the town, called Fort Volney after its commander, and Timberline was also the main source of supplies and entertainment for the three hundred soldiers stationed there.

Faro had met Hobart Nye, the timber-business promoter, in the bar of the Fremont Hotel shortly after his arrival in Timberline. As soon as Nye determined that Faro might be carrying a considerable amount of cash with him, he began to court the gambler with the idea of persuading him to invest in a logging operation in his thousand-acre redwood holdings. From the start Faro had no interest in the project, but he saw two good reasons for letting the little man believe otherwise. For one thing, Nye was a spender. After the first couple of days of their acquaintance, Faro quit even offering to pick up the tab for a round of drinks or a meal. Nye eagerly paid for everything. And, in addition, Nye offered to lead Faro on a tour of three or four successful logging operations to the north of the town in order to show him how the business worked. Along the way, Faro knew, he would be able to show some of the loggers in the camps how *his* business operated, too.

Chapter Two

The broad, confident smile had been obliterated from the features of Hobart Nye by the time he and Faro Blake returned to Timberline a few days later. After a profitable tour of the lumber camps to the north, Faro had disclosed his lack of interest in Nye's enterprises during the ride back to town. He had never made any commitments, Faro pointed out, and he had never tried to hide the facts that he was a gambler, not an entrepreneur, and that he was simply passing through on his way north. Any hopes that Nye had of getting his hands on the cash Faro carried had been manufactured completely in the diminutive promoter's mind.

Nonetheless they parted on a sour note when they reached Timberline. Nye still felt that he had been unjustly deceived and was bitter about the waste of time and lack of profit from the trip. After stabling his horse and stopping by the Fremont Hotel for a late lunch,

Faro wandered over to the saloon where he had done much of his gambling while in town.

The Redwood Roundup was the largest of the eight saloons in the town, and soon after his arrival in Timberline Faro had quickly selected it as the best place for him to set up shop. Not only did the Redwood have the only roulette wheel in town, but it also had the best selection of girls to be found anywhere north of Enterprise. Those two advantages alone were enough to ensure that the Redwood always drew more than its proportionate amount of business whenever the loggers or the troopers from nearby Fort Volney came to town to blow their pay.

Now in early afternoon the place was practically empty, but the staff was busy making preparations for the onslaught which was expected later in the evening. The army paymaster had visited the fort two days earlier, but tonight, a Friday night, would be the first chance the soldiers got to draw passes and ride into town. Sharp, the saloon's head bartender, was carrying cases of whiskey and kegs of beer from a storage room and placing them behind the long bar, and a shuffling, derelict swamper was at work with a mop and pail toward the back of the room.

Faro got himself a glass of whiskey and carried it to a side table out of the swamper's way. Some days before, he had made arrangements with the saloon's manager to operate his faro layout here in the Redwood for a flat five percent share of his winnings, but he had been gone for a while now and he wanted to check with the management and see if the same deal was still acceptable.

After about fifteen minutes Henry Sorbitt, manager of the Redwood, came in the front batwing doors and went over to the bar to talk to Sharp. Then in a moment, when he saw Faro sitting off to the side, he came over and took a seat across the table from him.

"I heard you were back, Blake," Sorbitt said. "I ran into Hobart Nye down the street a piece, and when I asked him how the trip went, his face got red as a tomato and I'd swear I saw a little steam shooting out his ears." Sorbitt was a tall man in his late forties with an open, friendly way about him and a quick sense of humor which made him popular with most of the patrons of the Redwood. But Faro knew he was a man who bore constant casual observation, too—Sorbitt had a penchant for practical jokes of all kinds, and in the brief time that Faro had been around him, he had learned that nobody was safe from his pranks. And yet Faro still liked doing business in the Redwood because Sorbitt ran straight games and preferred to give his patrons their money's worth, rather than bilking them with crooked tables and watered-down liquor.

"That's the breaks," Faro told him easily. "From the start I was a poor prospect for him, but he didn't seem to have sense enough to see it. I wouldn't want to risk my stake on a man whose judgment is that bad."

Sorbitt chuckled at the ironic logic in Faro's words. "Anyways, Blake," he said, "I'm glad you're back. Art Bunster that runs my roulette wheel for me is laid up with a broke hand, and I thought I might be able to talk you into handling the wheel for a few days 'til he gets back."

"It's not my game, Henry," Faro told him. "I've always been partial to the game my mama took my name from."

"I'd consider it a big personal favor," Sorbitt went on a little more insistently, "and it wouldn't be but for two or three days, four at the most. I'll pay you ten dollars a night and a third of the house take. That's the deal I made with Bunster."

Faro considered the matter a moment. He really didn't care for roulette. The betting table was a pain in the ass to manage, and there were too many ways to gimmick a wheel. But during the times he had been here during peak business hours he had seen how busy the roulette wheel stayed, and a third of the take was an attractive offer.

"Okay, I'll do it," Faro said. "I'll want to check the wheel over first, though. No offense meant, but I don't like the idea of stopping a hunk of lead because of somebody else's shenanigans."

"Hell, tear it down and check it over piece by piece if you want to, Faro," Sorbitt said. "It don't make me no nevermind, just so you got it back together and ready to spin by eight tonight."

As soon as their conversation was finished and the saloon manager had left, Faro went across the room to the big wheel to check it out. His first step was to check the floor for any loose boards under which a pedal might be hidden. Then he stooped down and examined the underside of the table, looking for any concealed buttons or wires. Finally he lifted up the large, free-spinning wheel itself and checked for any sign of magnets or tampering.

When at last he was satisfied that the wheel was straight and that he would not be unknowingly running a crooked game, he lifted the big wheel up and was about to set it back in place. But then a voice from nearby asked, "Did you check for a friction drag on the center-shaft bearings?"

Faro turned and looked quizzically at the stranger nearby. He had never heard of such a thing and wondered for an instant if the man intended the question as some sort of joke.

"It's harder to put in and not as reliable as a magnet," the stranger said, "but it does up the house odds, and not one in ten thousand men would know to check for it."

The man who sat at the table ten feet away calmly sipping from a tall mug of hot beer looked like anything but an expert on gambling devices. He was dressed in a shabby fringed buckskin shirt, brown wool pants, and scuffed-up black boots. He wore his hair long, but kept it out of his way with the aid of a wide leather headband tied around the top of his head. Faro judged him to be about forty years old and a man who had lived much of his life in the out-of-doors. As he got up and ambled over toward the disassembled roulette wheel, he introduced himself as Jason Ashford, a civilian scout for the troops at Fort Volney.

"I've only seen it done one time," Ashford said, "and that was a few years ago at a casino in the south part of France. This French count or duke or something was sure he was being cheated, so he pulled out this fancy percussion dueling pistol and blasted the croupier right slap between the eyes. But then, after they took the wheel down and started checking it, they couldn't find any sign of tampering. Well, sir, that Frenchman was getting pretty regretful about what he'd done, until they finally pulled the center shaft out and checked the bearings around it. On one side they'd been fixed so they drug against the shaft and slowed the wheel down on that side."

Faro didn't know whether to believe the preposterous tale or not, but as Ashford spoke he was continuing to disassemble the underportion of the roulette wheel as if he'd been doing it all his life.

"Like I said," Ashford went on, "it wouldn't up the odds like magnets under the rim of the wheel would, but it is still a money-maker and it's a damn sight harder to detect than any other roulette gimmick I've ever seen." Finally he lifted the center shaft up from the table and probed down into the hole with his fingers. He considered the matter for a moment, then turned to Faro and said, "Feels okay to me. I'd say you got an honest wheel here."

After they had the roulette wheel reassembled, Faro offered to buy Ashford a drink and they wandered off to a table on the far side of the room to talk.

"When you first started talking about all that bearing business," Faro admitted, "I thought you were greening me. You don't exactly look the part of an expert on gambling machines, nor, for that matter, much of a world traveler, either."

"Fact is, I did see it all just like I told you," Ashford assured him with an easy grin. "Looks can often deceive, my friend."

"Obviously," Faro told him. "But that still doesn't help a body understand any clearer what a man that used to hobnob·with counts and suchlike in Europe would be doing in an out-of-the-way place like this."

"Oh, that's simple," Ashford said. "I'm here because I like it here, and I'm doing what I do because I like that, too. How many men do you know who could say as much?"

"Not a one comes to mind right off," Faro admitted.

"When I first come across the Rockies, I was twelve years old," Ashford said. "That was in forty-nine, and me and Pa was out to strike it rich in the gold fields around Sutter's Fort, just like two or three hundred thousand other blasted fools from the States. Well, sir, Pa died that first year of the fever, and since I was too young to prospect on my own, I made my way killing game in the mountains and selling it to the miners who were too busy to scare up their own meat."

Faro leaned back in his chair and signaled Sharp for another round. This had all the makings of a long-winded life story. But what the hell, he thought. It was hardly five o'clock, and things would not get rolling in the saloon for another three hours yet.

"Time I was sixteen," Ashford went on, "I was tough as a panther, and I knew these north California mountains like the palm of my hand. About that time I decided to lie about my age and join up with the U.S. Army. I stayed in the service sixteen years. I came out of the war a captain, and by the time they drummed me out in sixty-nine, I'd already made major."

"After all that time, you must have done something pretty awful to get the boot," Faro commented with casual interest.

"They got a fancy word for it—insubordination—but what it all boils down to is one day I up and told General Crook to get fucked. We were up in the Dakotas at the time, trying to get the Crows to stop raiding the settlements along the frontier and to move farther west ino the wilderness. In August of sixty-nine Crook sent me and my company out with orders to wipe out a village of hostiles we'd located, but I knew it was full of women and children and old people, and I didn't have no stomach for that sort of doings. A week after Crook got my message, I got the sack.

"Back then I had me a little money saved up, and I decided I'd see some of the world with it. I spent a year in England, and two more on the Continent, mostly just roaming around and seeing how other folks went about living their lives out. But then one day it hit me. I wasn't happy where I was at, and I hadn't really been very content with anything I'd been doing for the last twenty years. The most happy and free I'd ever been was when I was on my own in the mountains of California, meat hunting for the gold miners. I packed my trunk the same day, and within a week I'd booked passage on a ship which was headed across the Atlantic, around the Horn toward San Francisco."

"It wasn't the same when you got back, though, I bet," Faro prompted him.

"No, it couldn't be," Ashford admitted. "But I've been content here for the last couple of years. I knew the country hereabouts well enough to hire on as a scout with the Army in these parts, so that puts me out in the wilds and moving around most of the time. It's only lately that things have begun to go haywire again, what with this new Indian trouble and all . . ."

"I haven't heard about any Indian problems in these parts," Faro said with rising interest. "Matter of fact, I didn't even think there was any Indians hereabouts to cause problems."

"Have you ever heard of the Leatherfoot tribe?" Ashford asked.

"Seems like I caught a piece in the Frisco papers some time back about them," Faro said vaguely. "It was something about a relocation project, I think."

"That's right. About six months ago the ranchers and settlers west of here in the Mako Lake region convinced the government that the Leatherfoot Indians would be happier off on a remote reservation up in Oregon than they were right here on their ancestral lands. Of course at the time nothing was said about the beautiful little valley which the Indians lived in north of Mako Lake, but days after they were moved away there was the biggest land rush up there that this part of the state has seen in twenty years.

"After that things were fine for a while. Out of sight, out of mind, and all that kind of bullshit. But nobody bothered to consider that on their new reservation home, the two hundred Leatherfoot Indians were open to attack by several hundred braves from a hereditary enemy tribe, the Klamaths. And on the east they were easy prey for an offshoot branch of the Nez Perces.

"About two months ago Major Volney out at the fort received word that the Leatherfoot had left the reservation. The local Indian agent up there had no idea when they had gone or which direction they headed. He just knew that every man, woman, dog, and horse had vanished. I'll tell you, when Volney got that message, his asshole tightened up like a wet cinch on a hot day."

"Well, has anybody figured out yet which way they went?" Faro asked.

"Maybe," Ashford said evasively. "Three months ago I would have bet my horse and saddle that I could lead you right to their camp on the first try, but that was before Burning Wind came."

"What do you mean by that? Who's Burning Wind?"

"I don't even know that for sure," Ashford admitted. The more he explained things, Faro thought, the less sense he made. "A few weeks ago, just before the Leatherfoot left the reservation, talk began about how a new chief had taken over leadership of the tribe. His name was said to be Burning Wind, but nobody seemed to know where in the hell he came from, and to my knowledge, no white man has even laid eyes on him to know what he looks like."

"It's like the Indian Messiah rumors that sweep through the Plains tribes every few years," Faro commented.

"That's exactly the way it is on a small scale," Ashford agreed. "Before Burning Wind, the Leatherfoot never raised a hand to protest anything the white men did to them. Their tribal lands were stolen piece by piece, and every time they just stood by and watched it happen, either too cautious or too afraid to ever fight back. And they finally let the army come in and take everything away from them and ship them off into the middle of hostile territory, and still they did not try to resist. But when Burning Wind came, all that changed. Within a matter of days they had jumped the reservation, and over the last couple of weeks there's been rumors circulating that they've come back to northern California, demanding that a binding treaty be signed and that they be given their land back. The settlers west of here are sweating bullets, especially those that moved in and grabbed the land north of Mako Lake."

Despite his job as a scout for the army, it was obvious that Ashford had more than a little sympathy for the Indians and that he was deriving a great deal of personal enjoyment out of this situation. He seemed to relish the thought that a mere two hundred unwarlike Indians could defy the entire United States government and terrorize the white residents of several hundred square miles of territory without even showing their faces or firing the first shot.

"Volney keeps me out on the move most of the time trying to find where they're at," Ashford said. "But so far I haven't turned up a clue."

"Hell, a tribe that small could camp on a quarter of an acre or less," Faro said.

"You bet they could. And I expect that right now they're staying on the move most of the time, sticking to some of the wildest country they can find," Ashford said. Then he added candidly, "That's why I spend about two-thirds of my time right here in town. I've got Volney believing that I can do more good by talking to travelers and staying up on the rumors of the loggers than if I was out there in the wilds looking on my own."

The two of them sat talking for a while longer, but when the saloon girls finally started filtering downstairs about six thirty for their evening's work, Faro began to find it harder and harder to concentrate on the plight of Indian tribes and the fears of remote settlers that he had never met and didn't particularly care to.

One certain young woman, a dark-eyed vixen named Lula, immediately caught Faro's attention, and soon she began devoting much of her time to teasing and tantalizing him, all the while acting as if she had yet to even recognize his presence in the room.

She had one of those slim, voluptuous bodies which always particularly appealed to Faro. Her breasts were round and full, ever threatening to spill out the top of the black silk chemisette which she wore, and it was obvious that the lacy red corset which she had around her middle was for effect and not because she needed it. The honey color of her long, slender legs was complemented perfectly by her red net stockings, and the high-heeled shoes she wore made her seem sensuously sleek and tall.

Lula was pretty in a bawdy sort of way. When she smiled, her tongue always seemed to be flickering around in the background, eager to go to work, and in a single flashing glance she seemed to have the power to communicate all sorts of salacious messages.

Soon Ashford began to realize that the conversation he was making could not compete successfully for Faro's attention any longer. He slugged back the rest of the beer in his mug and said, "Well, thanks for the beer, Faro. I figure I've bent your ear long enough with all this local gossip."

"I swear, that woman . . . !" Faro said distractedly. His attention was fixed across the room, and Ashford turned to see what it was that had inspired the exclamation. Lula was standing at a table about twenty feet away, her foot up on the seat of a chair as she leaned forward to straighten the wrinkle out of a stocking. At that angle, a creamy expanse of upper breast was enticingly exposed.

"I wonder what in the hell holds them in," Ashford pondered with a soft chuckle.

"It beats all hell out of me," Faro mumbled. "But I do think the situation merits further investigation."

Lula, who had been watching them examine her form, knew that the hook was set and that the fish was as good as caught. She raised up and turned away to talk to another of the girls nearby, but in a moment Faro had said his farewells to Ashford and was on his way across the room toward her.

Not bothering with any unnecessary preliminaries, he took her hand in his and said, "Come on, gal. I got me an itch that needs scratching."

As they started across toward the stairs which led to the second-floor rooms where the girls entertained their customers in private, Lula grumbled, "Well, ain't you the smooth one with the ladies! Won't you even buy me a drink and ask me proper before you go hauling me off for a humping?"

"If you were a damn lady," Faro told her lightly, "then we wouldn't be taking this little stroll in the first place. But you ain't, and I ain't no gentleman, neither, which means that the two of us are about to have a hell of a lot more fun than their kind ever even thought of having."

Soon after they reached Lula's room, she had her scanty outfit off and was sitting naked on the edge of the bed waiting for him by the time Faro got his jacket off and was beginning to unbutton his white frilled shirt. And by the bright smile of anticipation which lit her features, she seemed to like all that she was seeing as more and more of Faro came into view. Out of the suit and shirt which easily identified his gambler's profession, Faro Blake had the well-toned physique of a

boxer. The muscles of his husky, six-foot frame were
well defined and firm, and he moved with a smooth
agility that hinted at speed and good coordination. His
chest and upper belly were covered with a thick mat
of hair which matched the brownish-blond shade of
the hair on his head and the mustache which covered
his upper lip.

Though Faro never considered anything about his
looks particularly striking or handsome, many women
seemed to find his face fascinating. His jaw was broad
and firm, and his eyes had a certain penetrating gaze
which could within an instant change his whole expression from one of twinkling amusement to firm determination or seething anger.

All the while he had been undressing, Lula had been
marking his progress with her eyes, and when at last
he dropped his trousers and cotton drawers to the floor,
she let out a soft sigh of appreciation.

"I can see why you were in such a hurry to get up
here," she told him with a light laugh. "This swelling
of yours definitely needs some quick tending to." She
reached out and got herself a handful of his personals,
then pulled him toward her with gentle insistency.

"I've found out it's better to work off some of the
sexual tensions before I try to begin a busy night's
work," Faro told her. "Elsewise, if I had to spend a
whole evening trying to concentrate with a covey of
almost dressed females running around that looks as
good as you do . . ."

His little speech was cut short as she leaned forward from her seat on the bed and settled her warm,
moist lips over him. A shuddering chill of delight raced
the length of his body, and he had to brace himself
with his hands on her shoulders to keep from losing
his balance and staggering away. "Ummmmassogoo,"

Faro muttered, the sounds barely squeezing by the constriction in his throat.

Her skillful mouth and tongue manipulated him for a few moments, but then, just as he reached the very brink of finishing, she withdrew and her fingers tightened down firmly over him to prevent the final rush of pleasure.

"You're not getting off that easy, buster," she said as she turned her smiling face up toward him. "I'm going to have me some, too." She lay back on the bed, pulling him more roughly and demandingly toward her now, and Faro readily complied with her.

It was all over in a matter of minutes, as each of them knew it would be. Both of them knew their business and, simply put, there was no good reason for them to dawdle about getting what they had come here after.

Later, as Faro was pulling on his clothes again, he told Lula, "Thank you, darlin'. Now I'm ready to give 'em hell on that roulette wheel." He was smiling broadly, still enjoying that subtle feeling of contentment which usually followed a satisfying roll in the sack.

Lula was lingering on the bed, still naked and apparently not quite ready to get dressed and go back downstairs. The lovely mounds on her chest rose and fell in rhythm with her soft breathing, and as Faro gazed down at her for a moment before leaving he thought that it wouldn't take any huge amount of encouragement to get him to stay around for a rematch. But beyond the closed door the noise of loud talk and laughter was increasing. Duty called.

When he was fully dressed, he pulled a five-dollar gold piece out of his pocket, and Lula giggled as the cold coin dropped on the warm flesh between her breasts. "That's extra, just for you," he said. "I'll square the rest with Sharp when I go down."

"Okay, baby," Lula said. "And maybe when we get off work, if I don't feel too used up . . ."

At the door Faro turned and winked back at her before going out.

Chapter Three

A dozen soldiers and perhaps half that many other men were waiting impatiently to risk their wages on the turn of the big wheel by the time Faro drew his bank from the bartender and stepped behind the roulette wheel. Elsewhere in the Redwood Roundup as many as fifty or sixty other men were trying their hands at poker, paying lecherous courtship to the half-dozen saloon girls on duty, or simply sitting and standing around enjoying drinks and conversation with their companions. A full two thirds of them were in the simple blue uniforms of army enlisted men, and most of the rest had the familiar flannel shirts and knit caps of loggers.

Faro recognized it as a volatile kind of situation. Soldiers and lumberjacks got along in the same place about as well as bulls and bears, and with the catalyst of alcohol to turn little slights into big ones and grease rising tempers, practically anything could happen. But the unspoken agreement here in the Redwood seemed to be that whenever trouble began, the antagonists were quickly shuffled outside, where the only things that could be broken were human bones.

The crowd around the roulette wheel was roisterous and eager as Faro put his tin-box bank on the shelf below the wheel and turned to explain a couple of things to the potential players.

"All right, boys," he said, "most of you have probably already heard the house rules a dozen times before, but I'll run through them anyway. There's a hundred-dollar limit on first bets, and a thousand-dollar limit on letting bets ride. No leaning on the table, and no placing bets after the wheel's in motion. We don't take markers under any circumstances. The only things that count on the betting board are hard U.S. currency and house chips, and as far as we're concerned, if you haven't got the cash on you, you haven't got it at all."

"When you gonna quit preachin' and spin the fucking wheel, tinhorn?" one of the soldiers asked. He was a big, hulking bruiser with a mashed-in face like a Boston bulldog's. On the sleeve of his uniform were three broad yellow stripes which proclaimed that he was a buck sergeant.

"As soon as I see enough money go down to make it worth my time," Faro said calmly. He could see it was going to be one of those nights.

In a moment about a dozen men had put their money down on the various numbered squares and Faro closed the betting for the first spin of the wheel. He grabbed the wheel and gave it a quick clockwise spin, then put the small steel ball in the rim and set it in motion in the opposite direction. But then an odd thing happened. Before the wheel had hardly slowed at all, the steel ball settled down unusually fast and remained in one place before it should have. When the wheel stopped at last, Faro saw that the ball was in one of the two automatic "house wins" slots on the rim.

Angry complaints and oaths began to rumble through the crowd of players, but Faro spoke up quickly to try to calm the men around him. "Don't worry, boys," he assured them. "I'm not going to gather up any of your bets until I make sure this wheel is working all right. I'll just call that a free spin and let your bets ride."

Hoping against hope, he set the wheel and steel ball in motion again, but again the steel ball settled down entirely too fast, and when the wheel stopped, he saw that it was again in the "house wins" slot.

"Jest what kind of empty-headed jackasses do you take us for, you cheatin' tinhorn son of a bitch?" the ugly sergeant demanded. "I don't mind losin' when it's on the square, but shit . . . !"

"Look, Sarge," Faro insisted. "I just checked this wheel over personally this afternoon and there wasn't a damn thing wrong with it. But obviously since then somebody's . . ." He had already snaked his right hand inside his jacket, going for the Reid's, but then he thought better of it and never brought it out. Every one of the dozen soldiers around him was armed with a military-issue sidearm, and his tiny little derringer was hardly a match for that kind of firepower.

"All your 'obviouslys' don't make a damn bit of difference up against what we jest seen here," the sergeant growled at him. "Here's what I think of your 'obviouslys.' "

His long right arm slashed out across the width of the table, and had Faro been only a slight bit slower in his reaction, he would have caught the full force of the blow in his face. Instead he dodged aside and caught the sergeant's wrist, then gave it a sharp twist, slamming the man painfully across the betting board. But in an instant the troopers were swarming him from all sides, and all his attempts to shout out explanations and denials were lost in the commotion made by the men who held him immobilized. As they dragged him bodily around the table and toward the door, Faro realized what serious and immediate danger he was in. This would not be the first time a hapless gambler, crooked or otherwise, had been taken from a saloon and summarily hanged by an irate mob of men who believed they had caught him cheating.

Once outside, a few of the men predictably began shouting for somebody to get a rope, but to Faro's great relief, it did not seem to be the will of the entire crowd that he be strung up so quickly. Sharp, the bartender, showed up briefly and tried to argue in Faro's behalf, but when one of the troopers shoved the barrel of a pistol in his belly and told him to butt out, he decided to do just that.

"If you're so sure I did something wrong, then call for the sheriff and get him to sort this whole thing out," Faro told the dogfaced sergeant, who was standing nearby.

"That pencil-pushing pussy?" the sergeant scoffed. "Shit, he'd have you out of jail and back in business before the rest of us got done telling him our side of things. Nope, there's only one way to handle your kind, and that's with a short rope and a long fall."

"All right, you bastard," Faro snarled at him furiously. "Then you and me'll finish this argument in hell!" With one tremendous jerk, he pulled his arms free from his captors and made a lunge for the sergeant. He figured that even if he could stay free for no more than a full second, it would be time enough to latch his fingers around the man's throat and turn his windpipe inside out. Hell, dying was pretty awful any way you looked at it, but at least if a man had to go, it ought to be for something he really did.

As quick as a bolt of lightning, the blow came out of nowhere. It was delivered to the back of his head at just the right angle and with just the proper amount of force, and before Faro Blake could follow through with his deadly designs on the sergeant, he was lying in a twisted heap in the middle of the main street of Timberline.

Somehow the word *headache* seemed inadequate to describe what was going on inside Faro's head. His awareness of the painful eruptions within his skull was his first indication that he had regained consciousness, and for what seemed like days he just lay there, examining with an almost detached interest how miserable he was. He had never realized before that pain could have colors, but there they were. The constant overall background pain seemed to be a pale blue, while the sharp stabs which came and went with startling frequency were a sort of cathouse red. And here and there were splotches and streaks of yellow and green which rippled across the canvas of his agony like spilled paint.

Other senses sluggishly began to function. He smelled dirt, manure, and the thick, fascinating odor of blood. Parts of his body were as cold and clammy as the flesh of a dead man, and other parts felt as if they were baking in an oven. The sound of his own irregular heartbeat thudded in his ears like a drum.

The place where he lay, wherever that was, was utterly dark, and somehow he found that terrifying on the most instinctive and primal level. It did not feel merely as if he were lying in the darkness, but more like he was wholly engulfed by it.

His hand probed out tentatively and encountered a coarse, irregular surface which he identified as tree bark. He raised up slightly, letting his hand rove higher and higher, until he verified that he was inside a log-walled room. Then, after struggling unsteadily to his feet, he made his way around the perimeter to identify its dimensions. The ten-foot-square chamber had four log walls and one heavy plank door with a small barred window in it at about head height. Even before another door opened some distance away down a hall and an armed soldier started his way, he had already pretty well figured out where he was.

The soldier paused outside the door but could not see Faro standing just inside because of the darkness. "Blake?" the man called out. "How about it, Blake?"

"I'm here," Faro told him. The sound of both their voices rumbled through his head like an earthquake.

"When I open this door, you'd be smart not to try nothin'," the soldier cautioned him tensely. "The major's sent me over to fetch you to his office."

"The way my head feels right now, soldier boy," Faro assured him, "I wouldn't feel like starting a fracas with your eighty-year-old grandmother. Open 'er up."

The soldier let Faro out of the cell, then kept him covered with a service revolver as they marched the length of the hall and out the door at the end. As they went up half a dozen stone steps and out into the full light of day, Faro realized the reason for the oppressive darkness and clammy coldness of the Fort Volney stockade. It was built underground, directly beneath one of the largest log buildings within the confines of the fort's walls. In his cell Faro had believed that it must be nighttime, but now, as the bright sunlight scorched his unaccustomed eyeballs, he realized that it was midafternoon.

The twenty-foot log walls of Fort Volney enclosed a plot of land about one hundred yards square. Parapets five feet from the top of the vertical pointed logs lined the inside of the walls all the way around, and

the log lookout towers at each of the four corners
sported light, stumpy fieldpieces. Various buildings
lined the insides of the walls practically all the way
around—to the north were the headquarters building,
commissary, and stables; to the west, the armory and
several individual cabins for the fort's officers; and to
the south was a long line of barracks for the enlisted
men. A bathhouse and outhouses in the southwest
corner served the needs of the officers and enlisted
men alike.

"This major that you're taking me to see," Faro
asked his escort, "would that be Major Volney?"

"It would be," the trooper said.

"Well, why does he want to see me?" Faro asked.
"And for that matter, what in the hell am I doing here
in the first place?"

"Ask him," the soldier replied. This fellow was a
pure gold mine of help and information!

Faro was ushered around a corner and back into the
same building, atop the stockade where he had been
imprisoned. As soon as they entered a small, tidy orderly room, a clerk there went through a door to the
side to tell the major that the prisoner had arrived. In
a few moments, Faro was ushered in to see the commander of the fort.

Even on first glance, it was easy to see that Major
Nehemiah Volney was damn near as military as a
man could get. Beyond the broad expanse of his large
walnut desk, the fort commander sat so stiff and
straight that Faro wondered if he might not have a
steel rod fastened to his backbone. His uniform was
crisp and immaculate, right down to the rigid creases
on his sleeves and the dazzling gleam of his polished
brass insignia. Sitting absolutely motionless with both
hands flat on the desk before him, he gazed up at
Faro as if he were examining some piece of filth

dredged up from the fort's cesspool and brought before him.

"You are the gambler, Blake, I presume," Volney said sternly.

"That's right," Faro told him. "And I figure you are the major, Volney."

"I am Major Nehemiah Volney, commander of this military post. You will address me as sir."

It was obvious that this man had an ego to match the size of one of Nye's giant redwood trees, which made sense when Faro thought about it. Any man that would build an army fort and then tack his own name onto it had to hold himself in pretty high esteem. But who Volney was and whatever grand things he might have accomplished in his life didn't make a damn bit of difference to Faro; all he was interested in was getting this matter cleared up and getting the hell back to Timberline. He had a little piece of unfinished business to talk over with Henry Sorbitt, or whoever else it was that had tampered with that blasted roulette wheel.

"I'll be more than happy to call you sir," Faro told him dryly. Then he added, "But I'll expect you to return the courtesy, Major."

"You're not in any position to be insubordinate, Blake," Volney growled at him, obviously irritated at the challenge to his authority. "After receiving the substantiated testimony of one of the men in my command, Sergeant Karl Dober, concerning your illegal and illicit gambling activities, I have decided to institute proceedings against you and bring you before a court-martial board on charges of—"

"Now, hold it!" Faro stormed out. "Wait just one damn minute, mister! In the first place, this whole thing has come about because somebody decided to play a stupid joke on me. And in the second place, I'm a civilian, so if any trumped-up charges are going to be brought against me, they're going to have to be trumped up in a civilian court, not a military one."

"You're wrong, Blake," Volney informed him. "Due to the recent Leatherfoot Indian uprising and the threat to the peace and stability of the civilian populace, a state of martial law has been declared in this region. And under the conditions of martial law, I am empowered to exercise jurisdiction over any matters, military or civil, which I believe have a bearing on the stability of this region."

"And a gimmicked roulette wheel affects the stability of this region?" Faro scoffed.

"Were my soldiers to lose substantial sums due to an illegal gambling device, morale would be affected, and as a result discipline would suffer."

Down below, Faro could feel the grip on his balls tighten. This lunatic really believed that what he was doing was right, and who was there around to convince him otherwise?

"As I was trying to tell you before," Volney continued, "court-martial proceedings will be instituted against you, and until they are begun you will remain confined in the stockade. I will try not to let my personal abhorrence of gambling and gamblers influence the outcome of this case, but I cannot be responsible if the officers on the board espouse the same viewpoint as their post commander."

Great! Faro thought. Just fucking great! Now he was up for another stint of undetermined length in that same musty, ten-foot-square coffin, and when he did get out again, it would be to face a court-martial board whose members he could hardly expect to be unaffected by the prudery of their senior officer. But it was obviously not a time for any more displays of defiance and anger. This character meant business, and he held not only the better hand, but the whole deck of cards!

"Look, Major," Faro reasoned. "This whole thing could be cleared up a lot faster if I had just about ten minutes to question the right people in town."

"It's not necessary. All the witnesses are soldiers assigned to this post. They will be available when we need them."

"Yes, but they don't realize what they saw!" Faro insisted. "Sure, the ball dropped dead in the 'house wins' slot two times running, but it was probably because somebody put a magnet in just the right place below the wheel, and . . ."

"I have no intention of trying this case right here in my office," Volney told him sternly. "Everything will be revealed at the proper time and before the proper authorities. In the meantime you will remain incarcerated in one of the cells below. . . ."

On the way back to his cell Faro smoldered inwardly over the ridiculous treatment he was receiving here. Nothing about the situation made sense, and nothing about Volney's intentions to railroad him through a trial even hinted at fairness or justice. He'd been had, plain and simple.

At the top of the stairs leading down to the stockade he paused a moment and looked around him in all directions as he filled his lungs with fresh air, knowing it might be a while before he had the chance to sample any again.

"Come on, prisoner," the guard grumbled at him. "Get moving."

"Just give me a minute, fella," Faro told him. "I want to get me a good taste of this fresh breathing air so I won't forget what it's like. The air down there is as thick as steam, and it smells like horseshit."

"It used to be a stable," the soldier explained, "until we found out that our mounts kept getting sick from staying down there too much."

"So Volney decided to just keep people there instead, huh?"

"Why not? Your kind don't count for nothin', anyway."

After an insistent prod in the ribs from the guard's revolver, Faro was about to start on down the steps, but just then he caught a glimpse of Jason Ashford riding through the partly opened gates of the fort.

"Wait," Faro said, stopping again and ignoring the threatening jabs along his spine by the soldier behind him. "I know that man."

"So what?" the soldier said. "Everybody hereabouts knows Ashford. He scouts for this outfit."

"But I need to talk to him," Faro said. He turned again and mounted a couple of the steps until the soldier's pistol was prodding heavily against his midsection.

"Get in there!" the guard demanded loudly. "Why, if the major was to look out his window and see the two of us stalling around on the steps like this . . ." He didn't have time to finish what he was saying before Faro made his sudden, unexpected play. With one hand he grabbed the barrel of the revolver and swept it to the side while his other hand lashed up and delivered a stunning backhanded blow to the young trooper's jaw. In an instant the soldier was sprawled out across the stairs, gazing up in surprise at Faro, who now held the revolver pointed down at him.

"I said I need to talk to Ashford," Faro barked at him, "and I mean it." He flung the revolver far out into the middle of the nearby parade grounds, then marched back up the stairs past the unprotesting guard. Ashford had started toward the hitch rail in front of the barracks on the far side of the compound, but when he heard Faro calling to him, he turned his head to see who it was. Then, when he recognized Faro, he reined his horse around and rode over to him.

"So there you are, Blake," Ashford said as he stepped to the ground and shook Faro's hand. "I heard that some of the soldiers from the fort started this way with you last night, but I wasn't too sure what they might have decided to do to you on the way from there to here."

"I don't have a recollection of none of it," Faro told him. "Somebody cold-cocked me right after they drug me out of the Redwood last night, and the next thing I knew, I was coming to in the dark on a dirt floor in a basement."

"I heard about what happened only this morning." Ashford told him. "Sorry I wasn't out and about to give you a hand last night, but I'd decided to log a few extra hours of sleep and I turned in early."

"You didn't happen to hear who set me up, did you?" Faro asked. "Soon's I get back to town, me and that fella are going to have to swap some licks."

"Henry Sorbitt told me this morning that he did it," the scout said. "He said it was your old friend Hobart Nye's idea in the first place, but Sorbitt, being the way he is, thought it would be a damn joke. He planned to be there to stop things before they went too far, though, but then Nye slipped another surprise in the game. When the two of them ate dinner together yesterday evening, Nye slipped some kind of knockout drops in Sorbitt's coffee, and by the time the shit started flying in the Redwood, Sorbitt was dead to the world in an upstairs room of the Fremont Hotel. All in all, Henry says it's one of the best pranks he's seen played since he got to Timberline. He was still laughing his ass off about it when I left town this morning to ride out here."

"I figure I'll persuade him to stop laughing right after I get back," Faro said.

"Well, don't take things too hard," Ashford told him. "I'll go in and tell Volney how the whole thing came about."

"I'd be much obliged, Jason."

While they were talking the young soldier had been easing around toward his discarded revolver, and when he finally retrieved it, he marched toward Faro and Ashford with renewed courage. As the young man drew near, Ashford turned to him and asked calmly, "You aiming to shoot somebody with that thing, son?"

"I figure I at least owe him a good rap across the noggin with it," the trooper said angrily, "but I don't think nobody would fault me if I just went ahead and winged him good."

"What for?" Ashford asked.

"Well, shit, Mr. Ashford! First he won't go inside the lockup, and then he turns around and knocks me down and takes my gun away. He's my prisoner, and I ain't about to let him escape."

"You got any plans of escaping, Faro?"

"Well, I can't say as I really gave it much thought one way or the other," Faro admitted. "But now there don't seem to be much call for it." Then, turning to the soldier, he added, "I guess I should apologize for all that business over there, but like I told you at the time, I needed to talk to Ashford. And anyway, if I had a mind to escape, I wouldn't need to take your gun away from you to do it. I've still got one of my own." He opened his suit jacket to reveal his Reid's derringer, still nestled in its convenient holster inside the coat. He had first discovered that he still had the tiny weapon on him while he was in Volney's office but had decided that the situation had not yet reached the desperate point of gunplay.

"Well, you keep your gun on this unpredictable cayuse awhile longer if you've got a mind to, trooper," Ashford told the young soldier. "But you're going to have to do it while we walk on over toward Major Volney's, 'cause that's where I'm taking him."

As Faro and Ashford turned and started off toward the post headquarters, the soldier stood gazing after them a moment in confusion. Finally he holstered his revolver, muttered a disgusted "Aw, hell!" and started away in a different direction.

While Faro impatiently waited in the orderly room, Ashford spent about fifteen minutes behind closed doors with the post commander. When the scout finally came out again, closing Volney's door behind him, he said, "Well, things are worked out, I think. Come on. I'll tell you about it on the way over to my quarters."

Once they were out of the headquarters and starting across the broad compound toward a row of barracks-like buildings along the opposite wall, Ashford was able to speak more freely. "Before I tell you anything else, my friend," the scout began, "you're going to have to understand what a queer duck this Volney is."

"Yeah, I got a hint of that when I was in with him earlier," Faro said. "He thinks mighty well of himself, don't he?"

"He sure does," Ashford confirmed. "But after being around him for two years now, I've pretty well learned how to handle him."

"So am I in the clear, Jason? Can I get the hell out of this place now?"

"Well, not exactly, Faro. I told him about Nye and Sorbitt and how the wheel was rigged, but I don't think I ever really got the point across that you were just a victim ot this mess and nothing more. It seems like you smart-mouthed him pretty good when you were first in there, so he kinda wants you to be guilty of something."

"Well, shit, Jason . . ." Faro began.

"Now, hold on, Faro. Hold on," Ashford said. "There's not going to be any court-martial or trial or anything. At least, it's not definitely in the works like it was before. But he still wanted to keep you in the lockup for a few days longer until he got the chance to rehash things in his mind and talk to a few more people. Then's when I decided I'd try to convince him what a valuable man you could be to us if you got a little better treatment and weren't just pitched into a hole in the ground like some kind of common criminal."

A puzzled look came over Faro's face when his companion said that. If the situation came up, he had nothing really strong against the idea of helping the army, but he could not see how he could be of any possible use to the garrison here, short of picking up a rifle and going out to fiight the foe alongside them, which he was not about to do. Even back during the war he had felt no strong inclination to take up arms and join either side in the War Between the States, preferring rather to cross the lines freely and make his living gambling without prejudice with the troops from both the Confederate and Union armies.

"I think you're just going to have to trust me and play along for a while, Faro," Ashford continued. "What it all boils down to is that the man's definitely got it in for you right now. But if we string him along and make him think you'd be more useful on the loose than you would be behind bars, then I think we can change his opinion of you."

"You keep talking about how useful and valuable I can be," Faro said, "and that's the part I haven't got clear in my head yet. What could the army possibly need me for?"

"Well, I remember you telling me back in town about how you had traveled the country hereabouts a bit, running your faro layout in the different lumber camps and suchlike," Ashford said. "So I put the notion in Volney's head that a man who's seen that much of northern California must have a lot of valuable information stored up in his head. The commander of this post is an absolute fanatic about intelligence gathering. He seems to have the belief that if he knows about every rock and tree and stream for a couple of hundred miles around here, that will somehow make him a better soldier and will make the job of overseeing what's going on hereabouts somehow easier.

"And now, with the Leatherfeet back on the loose," Ashford continued, "he's really gone haywire. Any settler or trapper or ranch hand who makes the mistake of stopping by the fort here on his way to town is likely to go through a full-scale interrogation before he can get away again. That's why I thought it would be a good idea to mention your wanderings to Volney. He's bound to want to hear about every broken tree branch you noticed along every trail you rode, and, man, if you had by chance noticed any honest-to-goodness Indian sign, he'd probably present you with the key to the fort."

"I haven't seen anything, not any Indian sign or anything else," Faro insisted. "I don't see why I can't just get on my horse and ride."

"It's a bad idea," Ashford warned. "If you won't play it my way, I can't guarantee that you won't be sharing a cell in the basement with half a dozen rats as soon as you make your first wrong step."

"All right, all right," Faro conceded finally. It was

a damned lousy situation to be in, but at least living here aboveground beat the quarters he had been headed toward only half an hour ago.

They had reached the door to the small room which Ashford used on one end of a long log barracks, but just before they went in Faro happened to glance to the side. There, no more than fifty yards away, carrying a pail of water from the fort's well to one of the small homes used by the officers at Fort Volney, was one of the most stunning women he had seen since leaving Frisco.

Her flaming red hair was the color of maple leaves in the fall, and the features of her face were finely formed and gorgeous. Even at that distance, Faro could get an idea of how full and inviting her figure was beneath the simple calico dress she wore. She looked to be about thirty years old, and just reaching the prime of her womanhood.

Ashley, standing halfway in the door to his room, looked around and saw Faro studying the woman with intense appreciation. "She's Volney's wife," he said. "Forget it."

That's easy to say, Faro thought as the woman disappeared inside the front door of her home, but perhaps not so easily done.

Chapter Four

More than anything else, life at Fort Volney was utterly boring. The day began for the soldiers in the command at four every morning, and even the people such as Faro and Ashford who did not have to get up and hurry to the four-thirty formations in the center of the parade grounds were effectively roused by the blaring bugles, shouted commands, and formal reports which marked the daily ritual of military life.

Due to Volney's rigid set of personal scruples, there was, of course, no gambling permitted within the confines of the fort, and equally infuriating was the unavailability of any sort of alcoholic beverage. For his first couple of days there, Faro did little but peruse Ashford's dog-eared library of dime western novels with profound uninterest and linger for hours in a chair outside the door of Ashford's quarters, treasuring the occasional glimpses of Marantha Volney which he got.

After the first couple of times when the beautiful redhead noticed Faro watching her from his vantage point near the barracks, it seemed that her household duties took her much more often across the parade grounds directly in front of him. And though it would have been impossible to know what thoughts were behind the bright smiles which she occasionally flashed in his direction, he let his imagination go to work on the subject, with delightful results.

After supper on the evening of the second day, as Faro and Ashford were settling down in the scout's quarters to pass another dull evening, Ashford produced a worn deck of cards from under his mattress and suggested that if they drew the curtains over the windows and bolted the door, they might get away with playing a few hands of poker. Faro leaped at the idea, eager for any sort of entertaining diversion.

They played with dried beans for chips and the betting soon ranged into the hundreds and thousands of dollars, and the nicest thing about it was that when either of them lost his entire fortune to his opponent, he had only to dip into the nearby bag of beans for a new stake. Ashford played with surprising skill and knowledge of the game, and Faro quickly determined that the scout would be a tough man to go up against in a real, high-stakes game. He had no noticeable mannerisms which indicated when he was dealt good hands and when he was not, and the calm expression never left his face even in the midst of the most outrageous bluffs.

But Faro could also tell that only a portion of Ashford's thoughts was on the game they were playing. A melancholy sort of mood seemed to have overtaken him this evening, and for a long time the only conversation that passed between them was the monotone comments about the hands they were dealt. That was all right, though. A man needed some time occasionally to reflect on his own life and to mull over the way things were.

But finally a random comment by Faro struck a particular chord in Ashford and set him to discussing what he had been brooding over all this time. "You been here at the fort for two full days now," Faro said, "so I bet Volney is about ready to send you back out on the hunt."

"He don't know whether to shit or git," Ashford said with scorn. "He'd love to have me out there in the bushes full time, looking for cold campfires and moccasin prints, but he's afraid that if I'm away, some hot lead might come in and he won't have me on hand to guide him."

"Where would you rather be?" Faro asked.

"Damned if I know, either," the scout said sullenly. "When I'm out there lookin' I'm always wondering if Volney might launch out on some crackbrained campaign while I'm gone. But when I'm back here I just feel cooped up and useless, and I can't get the thought out of my head that every extra day this thing goes on without being resolved, the problem just gets worse and worse.

"Hell, Faro, scouting and tracking Indians is about the only thing I know how to do well, and back in the Dakotas, I guarantee you, I've blasted my share of Sioux and Blackfoot warriors off their ponies. But I know these Leatherfoot people and I don't want to hit the warpath against them. They've never been warlike, even back twenty-five years ago when the tribe was much bigger and stronger. When I was just a towheaded boy trying to make my living in these woods, the Leatherfoot tribe called the whole northeast corner of California their home, and yet, when the white men started pouring in here, they welcomed them and gave them prime land to start their ranches and to build their homes. But just like everywhere else, no matter how much they gave up, it was never enough.

"If I knew where Burning Wind and his people were today," Ashford vowed, "I swear I wouldn't lead Volney and his troops out to attack them. It's a stupid hope, I guess, but I just keep thinking that there ought to be some way to end all this without a whole lot of people on both sides getting killed."

Faro didn't say anything. From all he had heard and seen of past confrontations between Indians and white people, Ashford's hope was truly an empty one.

"One way or another, I guess," Ashford said, "these redskins are doomed, just like so many other tribes across the rest of the continent. They can only look forward to one of two fates—either they'll resist and be hunted down like coyotes for their efforts, or they'll give up all their ancient ways and change their very natures in order to get along in the world of white men. But either way, the Leatherfoot tribe will be no more."

"Maybe it wouldn't be such a bad thing to happen," Faro said. "I mean being sucked into the white world and all. Hell, it'd beat extermination, wouldn't it? And after all, we palefaces ain't got it so bad most times."

"Yes, but this is *our* way, not theirs," Ashford argued. "If the tables were turned, how would you like to face the prospect of being overpowered by a tribe of Indians and living the way they choose to live for the rest of your natural days?"

"I can't say as I'd place too much store by eating dog meat and sleeping in a skin tent in the dead of winter," Faro conceded, "although I do hear that Indians are mighty fond of gambling, which would suit my fancy to a fare-thee-well."

"Some years ago in Europe," Ashford said, "I occasioned to meet a young Indian man named Iron Deer from one of the American coastal tribes. At a young age he'd been taken away from his tribe and educated at some kind of holy-roly mission school, and he had shown such exceptional intelligence that the teachers secured a scholarship for him at Oxford. Even while he was in college he had started to invest his extra money in shipping, and by the time I met him he was a wealthy man. He dressed in the finest tailor-made suits and traveled in the fastest, most exclusive crowds in London, Paris, and Rome.

"Iron Deer spoke several languages, and was at ease in all kinds of circumstances and social situations. He had become a cultured world citizen, yes, but he wasn't an Indian anymore. All that fate had intended him to be had been stolen away from him, his ancestry, his heritage, everything. What was left was some kind of dandified, red-skinned sissy that had no idea of who he was or what kind of life he should be living."

Faro didn't interrupt or argue, because he could see that Ashford held some real mulish opinions along these lines, but he could imagine one hell of a lot of fates worse than being rich and living amongst the hoity-toity set in Europe. But he could easily agree with Ashford's notion that the Leatherfoot were getting a raw deal here. Maybe the American Indians shouldn't expect to control the massive tracts of wilderness that they once had before the white men came, but it seemed like they did have a right to some place where they could live out their lives like they wanted to. There was still a hell of a lot of open land here in the northern part of California, land that no white men wanted or considered worth the time it would take to clear it and put it to use, and with that in mind, surely there should be a place for a mere two hundred peaceful redskins from the tribe that had once owned it all.

Early the following morning Faro got wind that several wagons and a platoon of soldiers were going into Timberline that day to pick up a load of munitions and supplies which had recently arrived in town, and within a short time he had secured permission to go along. After Faro explained that he only wanted to pick up his valise and settle up at the hotel where he had been staying, Major Volney had no objections. With twenty soldiers along with him, it would be nearly impossible for Faro to get his hands on a horse and make it very far away from town without being caught and brought back.

The five-mile ride to town on the seat of a wagon was a fairly pleasant one. The countryside along the road alternated between open range land and cool, shadowy forest, and in two places they passed through groves of the towering redwood trees similar to the one on which Hobart Nye had staked his hopes. And the mere sight of the giant trees reminded Faro of the other reason he had for wanting to go to town. The Fremont Hotel was not the only place in town where he intended to settle up on unpaid debts.

When the group reached Timberline, as the military party headed off to pick up the supplies Faro walked to the livery stable where he had been keeping his horse and paid the several days of board which he owed. He planned to ride the animal back to the fort so that it would be available whenever the post commander finally decided to release him.

His next stop was the Fremont Hotel, where he paid his bill and picked up his valise and case of advantage tools. One of his biggest concerns during his confinement at Fort Volney was that somebody in Timberline would take it upon himself to look through his things for any reason. Inside the case of advantage tools was enough damning evidence to get half a dozen professional gamblers hung, and Faro knew he would be hard put to explain that the assorted marked decks, card trimmers, shiners, sleeve holdouts, and the like were not items which he routinely employed while at work.

But the fact was that most times he did not, as a matter of habit, feel the need to employ any of his cheating devices. Whenever possible, he preferred to make his living at the gaming tables simply by putting his superior knowledge and years of experience to work for him. But any man in his profession would be a fool not to have such advantage tools available to him when the need for them arose. To make a success in this business, even a straight gambler had to be as sharp as the cleverest shyster or crooked gambler he came up against, and some of the most enjoyable times in Faro's life were the few rare occasions when he had been able to end up one step ahead of some sharpie who had set out to put one over on him.

After his hotel bill was paid and the clerk had gone off into a back room on some errand, Faro took a moment in the deserted lobby to open the tool case and glance inside. Everything seemed to be just as he had left it, and he was greatly relieved to see that his stubby little sawed-off double-barreled shotgun had not been tampered with. It still rested snugly in its place, held along the side of the case by two leather straps, and far down in its barrels were the rolls of hundred-dollar bills which represented most of his fortune.

After strapping his gear on the back of the saddled horse, he led the animal down the street to the front of the Redwood Roundup and tied it to the rail there.

At this time of the morning, the front doors to the Roundup were still locked up, but Sharp was inside taking inventory and readily admitted Faro.

"Glad to see everything come out all right for you, Blake," the bartender told him as he drew Faro a beer from a keg behind the bar. "I wish I could have helped you out more the other night, but when the ruckus started, them troopers had me covered before I could get to the shotgun back behind the bar. And later on, they made it clear how dangerous trying to help you would be."

"You done right to back off, Sharp," Faro assured him. "It wasn't no healthy time to be identified as a friend of mine just then. Where's Henry Sorbitt?"

"He's down the street getting himself a bite," Sharp said. "But listen, Blake, if you're aiming to stir up some kind of fuss with him, I wisht you wouldn't. I might not always agree with the brand of hard jokes he goes in for, but it looks like things come out all right for you, so there ain't any use in more trouble coming from it."

"Hell, I know it was just a joke and I don't aim to give him no hard time over it," Faro said without the slightest trace of anger in his manner. "But I did lose a night's wages over it, and I figure he ought to pay me the cash money it cost me. How about rounding him up and telling him I'm here?"

"All right, I'll be right back," Sharp said. "Help yourself to another beer on the house if you're of a mind."

As soon as the bartender was out the front door, Faro went over to the roulette wheel and quickly began to take it apart. He knew it would not take Sharp long to round up Sorbitt and bring him back, but Faro knew exactly what he wanted to do and he believed he would have time enough to get it done.

Before leaving the fort that morning, Faro and Ashford had held another conversation about the manipulation of roulette wheels. It had occurred to Faro that if the mechanical parts could be gimmicked in such a way as to favor the house, why couldn't the same principle be used in reverse?

Within moments he had the wheel stripped down and had inserted a small shim into the main bearings. The little piece of wood was hardly thicker than a toothpick and only about half as long, and once Faro had it in place it could not be seen unless the whole bearing was pulled out and examined. But if he had placed it properly, Faro thought, then playing the roulette wheel at the Redwood would soon be a much more popular and profitable pastime for the soldiers and loggers who patronized the saloon. And with any luck, Sorbitt would be driven half crazy before he finally discovered what was going on.

By the time Sharp returned with his boss, Faro was back across the room, casually sipping from his mug of beer. The attitude of the saloon manager was still tentative; he was not yet convinced that Faro would not assault him, but Faro did everything he could to put Sorbitt at ease.

"Sharp says you ain't pissed about what happened the other night," Sorbitt said, advancing toward Faro with some caution.

"I wasn't exactly laughing my ass off when I come to in the stockade out there at Fort Volney," Faro admitted. "But then, when I thought about it some, I thought, 'What the hell?' I don't reckon you meant me no harm nor planned for things to go as far as they did."

"No, I shore didn't, Faro," Sorbitt admitted. "But it was a good laugh on all of us the way things turned out. Now I guess I'll have to stay on the lookout full time to see how you're going to get back at me, though, won't I?"

"Not for a while, at least," Faro said. "I'll be stickin' at the fort for a while, I guess, till the major out there decides I ain't a hazard to the community nor no kind of general public nuisance. It suits me, though. I'm getting plenty of rest and the eats are good."

When Faro left the Redwood Roundup a few minutes later, he was on the best of terms with Sorbitt, and he was also fifty dollars richer than he had been when he went in. The saloon manager had been easily persuaded to recompense Faro for the money he might have earned had he operated the roulette wheel for an entire evening.

The soldiers were already beginning to line up their loaded wagons at the end of the street in preparation for the trip back to the fort, but Faro knew he would still have a few more minutes before they were ready to leave. Each driver and horseman in the group would take the time for at least one drink in a nearby saloon before starting back to Fort Volney.

And a few minutes, Faro figured, maybe ten at the most, would be all the time he needed to take care of the last errand on his agenda.

Hobart Nye was leaned back in a chair asleep when Faro entered the office of Nye's Bear State Timber and Logging Corporation, located in a tiny second-floor room above the Timberline Meat Market. The cramped ten-by-ten office contained little but a couple of pieces of secondhand furniture, a large map on the wall with Nye's tract outlined on it in red ink, and a shitpot full of Nye's grand dreams and schemes. Faro quickly dealt with the matter of the little man's late-morning nap by kicking the chair out from under him and sprawling him in a confused tangle on the floor.

"Wake up, you weasel-faced little cocksucker," Faro said, glowering down at him. "It ain't nice to be asleep when company comes to call."

Nye didn't try to rise to his feet, probably realizing that he would be back down again almost as quickly as he got up. Instead he tried to play dumb, acting as if he had no idea why Faro would come in here and brutalize him so. "Why in the world did you go and do that, Mr. Blake?" the little man asked. "Have you lost all reason completely?"

"I'm on the point of it, Nye," Faro said. "That's how pissed off I am at you right now, you little shithead!"

"But why?" Nye asked. "I thought our association was concluded some days ago. What's made you so angry?"

"Well, you could start out with me being made a fool of in the Redwood the other night, and then just go right down the line from there. Getting hauled out in the street like a sack of meal, almost having my neck stretched, getting clopped across the skull with something that felt like a sixteen-pound sledge, having my ass locked up in a dark, wet hole in the ground . . . Is that enough, or do you want me to go on?"

Faro duly expected Nye to respond with all kinds of denials and pleas, but instead the little promoter's gaze shifted over toward the door and a sudden, calculating grin came over his face. Faro paused a moment, and then he noticed it, too—the sound of heavy footsteps on the stairs outside.

Faro glanced over his shoulder just in time to see a big, burly man open the office door and start inside. He had two brimming cups of coffee in his hand, and as he shoved the door aside with his leg he asked, "You wanted yours with sugar, right, Mr. Nye?"

But then almost immediately he saw Nye on the floor

with Faro standing above him, and a dark scowl passed onto his features. "Is this the man, Mr. Nye?" he asked.

"The very one, Lonzo," Nye said.

As the man named Lonzo crossed the room and set the cups of coffee down on the desk Faro began to take his measure, knowing what was likely to happen next. Lonzo was a good three or four inches taller than Faro, and perhaps seventy-five pounds heavier. His long, hairy arms looked as thick and substantial as railroad crossties, and he moved with a brutish, lumbering gait, like that of a giant grizzly that knows it is impregnable to attack by anything in the forest.

"How bad you want 'im hurt?" Lonzo asked. "For the same twenty dollars, you can get busted bones or jus' plenty of bumps and bruises."

There was only one practical way to deal with the situation, Faro decided as the bigger man started across the room toward him. His hand snaked inside his jacket to his vest, and when it reappeared an instant later, the trusty little Reid's derringer was cradled in the palm of his hand. But he hadn't really counted on any sort of participation from Nye, and when the little man made a lunge for the hand that held the gun, shoving Faro's arm off to the side, it was a complete surprise to Faro. The gun discharged harmlessly through the outside wall before flying from his hand, and Lonzo immediately closed the space between them. His huge hands swallowed up great wads of Faro's jacket and shirtfront, and Faro was lifted bodily off the floor and slammed hard against the closest convenient wall.

As Faro gagged, trying to suck some air back into his lungs, the big man asked again, "How bad, Mr. Nye?"

"Imagine you just caught him raping your fifteen-year-old sister," Nye said with a triumphant sneer, "and then take it on your own from there."

While one hand still held Faro pinned against the wall, his feet a good six inches off the floor, the man's other fist drew back about half the width of the room, then came barreling forward with the speed and impact of a steam locomotive. Faro threw up one arm, trying to deflect the blow, but only succeeded in lessening its force somewhat. The big fist glanced painfully off his jaw, sending a galaxy of stars racing across his vision. Then immediately, like a piston, the fist drew back and started forward again. Faro prepared himself for this one by dropping his chin down and letting the blow take him across the top of his head. He wasn't sure whether the dry crack he heard was bones breaking in his skull or in Lonzo's hand. But one thing he did know was that he definitely had to put a stop to this shit as soon as possible.

It took three direct kicks to Lonzo's crotch before his determination even began to falter, but by the time the fourth, fifth, and sixth blows had landed, the message was starting to get through to the big man that shortly he wasn't going to have anything but a bag of mush between his legs where his balls used to be. Roaring out his pain and frustration, he flung Faro away from him to put a halt to the agonizing assault. Then for a moment he stood in the center of the room, half doubled up and suddenly unsure of whether he wanted to continue on in Nye's employment or not. His hands had already dropped down instinctively to his offended personals, cradling them gently in an effort to lessen the pain.

Faro, still stunned and reeling from the two blows which had connected, was leaning up against a wall a few feet away, trying to muster enough sense and energy to defend himself if the fight continued. But soon he determined that Lonzo just wasn't in the mood anymore.

"I expect you already feel like you done twenty dollars' worth of fighting," Faro suggested.

"Mite near," Lonzo groaned out.

"Why don't we stop, then?"

"But he ain't paid me yet," Lonzo complained.

"Well, hell, friend!" Faro said. "If that's all that's worrying you . . ." He turned and snatched Hobart Nye to his feet by the collar of his coat, then held him out as if proffering a squirming, protesting gift to the big man. ". . . then take what you got coming. He keeps his folding money in the left inside pocket of his coat."

"We had a deal, Lonzo!" Nye squealed out in alarm. "You promised you'd take care of him for me. That's what you were to get paid for!"

"Hell, he racked my balls, Mr. Nye," Lonzo complained as he snaked a hand inside the little man's jacket and withdrew a cowhide wallet. "I'm through for the day. My stones is shooting fire clear up from my asshole to my earlobes."

"But, Lonzo!" Nye pleaded. "You can't just leave me here with him, especially not now! Not after this fight!"

"I reckon he can," Faro goaded the little man. Lonzo had already withdrawn his twenty dollars from Nye's wallet, but now he was eyeing the remaining cash with a great deal of interest. "Go ahead, friend," Faro urged him. "Considering how bad your seeds are paining you right now, I think you deserve a little bonus, don't you?"

Grinning broadly at last, Lonzo drew an extra twenty dollars from Nye's wallet, then pitched the wallet onto the desktop. He turned and went out the door, still bent forward and obviously in pain but forty dollars happier now than he had been a short while before.

When he was alone with Nye again, Faro retrieved

his derringer from the place where it had fallen, checked it briefly, and put it back in place under his jacket. Then he turned to see that Nye had backed clear across the room to the far wall. The entire left side of his face was a mass of nervous spasms and twitches, and the sweat which was pouring off his body had completely saturated his trousers, shirt, and jacket. Though he would not allow it to show on his features, Faro was enjoying the holy hell out of this moment.

As he advanced ominously across the room toward Nye, Faro asked, "Do you know what they do to gamblers when they catch them cheating, little man?"

Nye didn't answer. Faro hadn't expected him to.

"They hang them, most times," Faro said. "First the crowd gets real good and pissed, then somebody flings a rope over a tree limb or rafter, and they swing that sucker up there 'til his eyes bulge out and his tongue turns blue. If his neck don't snap clean right away, then he hangs there for a long time, strangling kinda slowlike. I've seen a man dangling at the end of a rope take up to eight, ten minutes to die, but I hear tell it can take twenty. It's plumb awful."

Nye nodded his head in agreement. He opened his mouth as if to speak, but no words came out.

"Yessir, there's something fascinating about a hanging," Faro went on. Calmly, as he continued, he reached around behind himself and pulled out of his back pocket the short coil of lariat which he had brought along. "Folks'll leave their crops in the field and ride fifty miles to see one, and then, when the feller's dead, they'll stand around for the longest time, just gawking at the way his feet turn kinda slowlike and imagining how it must feel to pass over that way. But I know one little belly-crawling skunk that ain't going to have to imagine no more."

"No! You're just trying to scare me," Nye said. His

voice was low and raspy now, and there was no conviction behind his words. "You ain't the kind of fellow to do such a thing over just a simple little joke!"

Faro held up the lariat to show Nye the slip-knotted loop he had been working on, then plastered his best evil grin across his face. "I'm a real son of a bitch when I wanta be," he said.

Suddenly Nye made a clumsy break for the door, but Faro had been expecting that for some time. Pivoting on the ball of his left foot, Faro swung with a hard roundhouse right, clipping Nye in the temple as he went past. It was a stunning blow but was not hard enough to knock the little man completely out.

While Nye was still down, his head addled by the punch, Faro set to work on him. First he pulled Nye's belt loose from around his waist and secured his hands behind his back with it. Then he ripped one lapel off the little man's jacket and succeeded in stuffing most of it into his mouth. And finally he pulled a handkerchief out of Nye's back pocket and tied it around his eyes.

"Seeing as how I didn't actually get my neck stretched as you intended," Faro told Nye, "I decided it was only fair to give you about the same kind of chance for a break that I had." He picked up the chair that Nye had been sitting on a while before and twisted two of the four legs off from opposite corners. "Hell, somebody might come up here ten minutes after I leave and save your hide," he continued, but then he added, "or might not anybody decide to check after you for days and days and days . . . not till the odor gets so ripe that they commence to smelling it down in the street."

He tied the loop of rope around Nye's neck and hauled him to his feet, then left him standing there, limp and whimpering, while he pulled the desk over to the center of the room. Using the desk to stand on, he took only a moment to get Nye in position atop the wobbling two-legged chair with the rope secured to a beam above him. When he had finished, the little man was suspended high enough so that only the balls of his feet were resting precariously on the chair.

After moving the desk out of the way, Faro stepped back and surveyed his work with satisfaction for a moment. "When you get to hell, tell all my friends down there to be on the lookout for me," he said. "But let them know I won't be making the trip anything like as soon as you'd hoped."

As he closed the door to Nye's office behind him and started down the stairs to the street Faro wondered with a chuckle how many hours of anguish Nye would go through before he finally toppled off the chair and discovered that the knot Faro had tied across the beam would not support his weight.

Chapter Five

"They got everything, my goods, my packs, my mule, and then before they left they even took my father's watch and fob. General, you got to do something!"

"It's Major Volney. *Major,*" Volney told the man, with a rising note of irritation in his voice. "Why in the hell can't you get that straight?"

"Captain, major, general, it's all the same! You're the army, aren't you? What are you going to do to get my goods back for me? What good is a trader if he has nothing left to sell?"

Faro had reached the headquarters building to report his return to the fort just in time to witness the report of this traveling trader, who had apparently been accosted and robbed by a band of Indians somewhere miles east of the fort.

By his accent, it was apparent that he was of Italian descent, a tall, darkly handsome man in his mid-thirties with a full Napoleon III beard and mustache. He wore a light, eastern-style suit, practically the standard uniform for an itinerant drummer of the day, and he explained that he had been visiting the small ranches and settlements to the east, marketing his line of assorted cooking vessels.

"Many times I have traveled this area," the man went on, gesturing emphatically as he spoke, "and everywhere I go, people know that Luigi Scirocco is a peaceful man, a fair trader who only wishes to be left alone to make his humble living in peace. But these wild red Indians, they have no respect. They steal from a poor but honest drummer who means them no harm . . ."

Scirocco had apparently reached the fort only a short time before the detail returned from town and had been immediately brought to the major's office where he could be interrogated by Volney and Ashford. When Faro came in a short time later, he entered the office uninvited, drawn by curiosity over what he heard from the adjoining orderly room.

"And you say this attack took place somewhere along the river road about halfway between here and Mako Lake?" Ashford asked.

"Two days ago in the dead of night," Scirocco said. "And since then I have been walking, walking, walking . . . two days I walked to come here to this place. They took my packs, they took my pots and pans, they took my mule, Benito, that I have owned for six years now and never had to beat to make him go . . ."

"Okay, okay, Mr. Scirocco," Volney said impatiently. The reported Indian sighting had him quite obviously excited, and all this irrelevant conversation by the trader was only increasing his agitation. "How many of them were there, and which way did they seem to be going? You must cooperate and tell us all you know if you expect us to do anything at all for you!"

"I was camped by a little stream called Bessler Creek, near where it goes into the Mako River," Scirocco told them. "There were at least a dozen of them, and their clothes were wet chest high, like maybe they had just finished fording the river from the north. When they left, they went south toward the river road, laughing and shouting and banging all my fine pots together. You know a pot with a dent, it's no good to nobody. Who wants to buy a pot with a dent, even for half price?" he mourned.

"Could you tell who their leader was?" Ashford asked. "What did he look like? What did he say?"

"There was no doubt," the trader said emphatically. "He was a big man, inches taller than all the rest. His eyes were like the devil's eyes, big and wild, and when he grinned it was horrible, like he could tear your throat out with his teeth and drink your blood. I was sure they would kill me, but instead they just took all I had and went off into the forest to the south."

"That has to be Burning Wind and his bunch," Volney said conclusively.

"It must be," Ashford agreed. "To my recollection, no Indians from any other tribe have roamed this far south in ten or fifteen years. The Klamaths seem pretty content up there on their reservations, and the Nez Perces have too many problems on their hands up north to wander down in this territory stirring up a fuss."

The interrogation of the trader continued on for some time, but eventually Faro lost interest and wandered out of the office. The sighting might have some special significance which escaped him, but he doubted it. It was no secret that when the Leatherfoot Indians jumped the reservation they would undoubtedly head in this direction, and so a single sighting should be no great surprise to anybody. And the mere fact that a dozen braves from the tribe had attacked this lone trader did not necessarily mean that the rest of the Leatherfeet were anywhere within fifty miles of the same location.

Volney might choose to muster his troops and take up the chase, but Faro had serious doubts that such an effort would be fruitful. For one thing, the trail would be at least three days old by the time they reached the spot where Scirocco had camped, and for another, the mere fact that they had headed south away from his camp when they left did not necessarily mean that was the direction they were traveling in.

He stopped by Ashford's room briefly to drop off his valise and case of gambling devices, then took out his shaving gear and started toward the fort's wash-house at the southwest corner of the stockade. With his gear left in town and him out here at the fort, it had been three days since Faro had had the opportunity to clean up and groom himself properly, and now would be a good time of day to take care of that, he thought, since most of the troops were on duty now at various other places around the fort.

He pumped one of the iron tubs full and took a bath, then padded out, still naked, into the large open area of the bathhouse where the men did their shaving and other grooming before a long row of tin-lined basins and mirrors. There he set to work whipping up a good lather with his shaving mug and brush, and he scarcely noticed when the door opened back to the side and somebody entered.

But then a voice said from the other side of the room, "I knew if you stayed here long enough we would meet eventually, but I had no idea that it would be under such revealing circumstances." Faro turned around, startled at the sound of a woman's voice, and saw the major's wife, Marantha Volney, standing near the door. With no visible signs of embarrassment, the woman was looking him over carefully from head to foot, seeming to take his measure both as a whole and by his separate parts. And to judge by the appreciative grin which soon crossed her features, he seemed to measure up in her estimation.

Though he was not particularly inclined to do so as a natural reaction, Faro decided at last that he'd better make at least a passing try at showing some modesty. If anyone were to step in here and see him standing there, buck-assed naked and with his vital organ standing up and saluting the major's wife, as it seemed very inclined to do at the moment, word might get around about the encounter. It would probably make a helluva bad impression on Volney when he heard and might land Faro back in the hole for his indiscretion. Reluctantly he took his trousers off the sink where they were lying and slipped them on.

"It's an odd place for it," Faro told her, "but I guess introductions are still in order. My name's Faro Blake, ma'am. I'm sort of a live-in guest around here right now."

"I know who you are, Mr. Blake," she told him, "just as I'm sure you know that I am Marantha Volney and that my husband is the commander of this post. And this is a remarkable coincidence, because I was telling Nehemiah just this morning that I would like to invite you and Mr. Ashford to dinner in our home."

"I'd be mighty pleased to accept that invitation about any time," Faro told her. "Right now time is something that I find myself with plenty of."

"Good," she told him with a bright smile. "Then we'll make it this evening, if that's agreeable to you."

She moved to one of the bath stalls in back, and for a delightful moment Faro thought she might be about to strip down and take a bath herself, and him right there, available and maybe willing to take the risk in case she needed somebody to scrub her back or perform some other vital service for her. But she reappeared a moment later, her arms loaded with several yards of flowered yellow calico material.

"I wonder if you might help me fold this back up," she asked. "I plan to make a new set of curtains out of **it,** but I had to wet it down and get the shrink out of it first. I've had it in there drying since this morning."

They stretched the material out between them across the bathhouse, and then Marantha started folding it up, working her way toward him. "It occurred to me a couple of days ago that you must be a man in need of a good, home-cooked meal," she told him lightly.

"It's a dead certainty that I'd enjoy one," Faro said, "but I wonder how you could know that much about me before we'd ever even met."

"Oh, it was easy," she said. "For the past few days, every time I came out of the house and saw you sitting there in front of the barracks, you had this terribly hungry look in your eye." By the look on her lovely smiling face, it was obvious that she knew as well as he did what it would take to satisfy that hunger, and it wasn't roast beef and potatoes.

She worked her way all the way across the room to him, but even when she had accepted the last of the cloth from him, she did not immediately move away. The smell of her perfume threaded its way into his nostrils enticingly, and at this angle it was an absolute chore to keep his eyes from plunging down the front of her dress in search of treasured glimpses of her voluptuous breasts.

"Thanks for the help," she said, casually touching his arm as she spoke. "Please tell Mr. Ashford about the invitation, and both of you come at eight. I know you and my husband are not on the best of terms right now, but don't worry. I still guarantee it will be an enjoyable experience for you."

"I don't have the slightest doubt about it." Faro grinned down.

He followed her with his eyes all the way out the door, mumbling to himself as he watched her swaying hips disappear from view. "Watch yourself, old son. There's nothing but trouble ahead when you start letting a hard dick call the shots."

But despite all his warnings to himself, he knew it was a lesson that even years of experience had failed to properly drum into his head.

The talk around the Volney dinner table that evening, as could logically be expected, centered mostly on the military situation and the Indian problems of north California. The major was still up in the air over the report received from Luigi Scirocco that afternoon, and it was all Ashford could do to steer him away from the notion of leading his whole command on a full-scale expedition eastward out the river road toward Mako Lake.

For Faro's part, he was content to keep his mouth shut and let the conversation go around him without taking any active part. Whatever had happened, would happen, or might happen that shouldn't, it was all out of his range of expertise or interest. He didn't mind playing the part of useful informant if it meant staying out of the fort's pokey in the process, but nobody could expect him to know anything about the lay of the land to the east, where he had never been and never particularly cared to go.

What did interest him, however, was the nonverbal kind of communication which Marantha Volney was doing with him while her husband's attention was tied up in other directions. Within the confines of the low-necked yellow dress she wore, her body was speaking a kind of language which was universally understood all over the world, and the signals she repeatedly flashed in his direction with her eyes were no less easy to comprehend. The message was simple and direct: "Let's fuck!"

But, although the spirit and the flesh were willing, Faro knew that the circumstances were anything but ideal. Fooling around with a married woman under any circumstances was a risky proposition at best, but when the woman's husband held your freedom and your future in his hands, the nŏtion was utter lunacy. And yet . . .

"More potatoes, Mr. Blake?" Marantha asked from across the table. As she made the offer she rose slightly out of her chair and held the dish out to him, almost begging him, it seemed, to take a gander down the front of her dress. Obliging her as best he could while he blindly scooped about half the bowl of potatoes onto his plate, he realized only after she sat back in her chair what a mistake he had made.

The potatoes, of all the dishes which comprised this awful meal, were positively the foulest-tasting things on the table. They had little gray flecks in them which Faro would not even take a shot at identifying, and the overall flavor might be closely matched with just the right combination of chalk, finely ground chili peppers, and horse liniment. She had identified the concoction as *poms de cribblers* or some kind of similar French-sounding name, but Faro took no pains to remember it; it was definitely not a dish he would be ordering in any French restaurant that he frequented from Frisco to Denver.

Other delights on the table included rubbery slabs of veal coated with sawdust and baked in a mustard-and-iodine sauce *(veau aw must),* a concoction of very suspect toadstools sautéed in butter *(champing yawn vert),* and of course the ever-favorite turnip casserole *(ragout de navit).* Not unexpectedly, all were Major Nehemiah Volney's favorite French dishes, churned up and dished out just the way he liked them.

And for Faro's part, he did his best at stashing away a respectable amount from his plate while repeatedly assuring Marantha that this was the best spread he had sat down to since the last time he put his feet under his mama's table some twenty-something years before.

Finally, during a pause in Volney's and Ashford's strategy discussion, Marantha decided to enter into the conversation around the table. "Nehemiah, since it looks like you'll soon go off chasing Indians all over the countryside and I might be cooped up here in the fort for some time, I think I'll make that trip into town that I've been putting off. I could leave first thing in the morning and easily be back here at the fort by noon."

"As you wish, my dear," Volney said to his wife.

"Mrs. Filpot, who stopped by here last week on her way back to her husband's ranch, told me of a delightful bolt of yard goods they have in the general store, and I think I might like to make a new set of curtains to brighten up this room. It's a lovely flowered yellow calico material that should go well with the yellows in the settee and the chintz lampshade."

Faro had begun to eye Marantha curiously by now. The material that she mentioned sounded suspiciously like the yards of cloth that she had soaked, shrunk, and enlisted Faro's help in folding up in the washhouse earlier in the day.

"It would be good for you to have some little project to work on in case this Indian business keeps us away from the fort for any extended time," Volney agreed.

"I'll tell First Sergeant Flaugherty to detail two men at tomorrow morning's formation to go with you."

"I don't think that will be necessary, darling," she answered brightly. "It just so happens that I ran into Mr. Blake today down at the bathhouse . . ."

Lord help me, he thought. *What's going to come out of this woman's mouth now?*

". . . He was coming out just as I was going in, and he happened to mention during our conversation that he still had some sort of banking transaction to do in town that he didn't get done today. It occurred to me then that it would be convenient for the two of us to ride together."

When Volney shifted his gaze unexpectedly toward Faro, he felt as if he didn't have much choice in the matter but to catch the stick Marantha had pitched him and run with it. To deny knowing anything about what she was talking about would make both of them look suspicious as hell. Besides that, he was beginning to see what Marantha Volney was working toward, and damned if the idea didn't seem like a good one.

"I generally try to deal with the head man in any bank where I do business," Faro explained with what he hoped was a poker expression. "But when I went into the Timberline Bank today, the president there, what was his name . . . ?"

"Oh, you mean Wilfred Posnick?" Marantha coached him.

"Yeah, Posnick was out with a touch of the bursitis in his shoulder. So I told them I would get back and see him later."

"I know Mr. Blake is supposed to be under confinement here at the fort," Marantha continued. She had obviously worked out every detail of this beforehand. "But he doesn't strike me at all as the kind of gentleman who would leave a lady stranded and without relief somewhere in the wilderness."

"Absolutely not," Faro said righteously. He had all kinds of relief just waiting to be delivered to this lovely lady across the table from him. As a matter of fact, his relief provider even at that very moment was rising up and responding to the call.

"I see no harm in it, my dear," Volney said at last. "Mr. Blake has shown no signs of being the unscrupulous culprit I first believed him to be, and Jason here speaks very highly of him. It should be a pleasant outing for the two of you."

Yes, very pleasant indeed, Faro thought.

He didn't get a whole lot of sleep that night. A host of rambunctious redheaded vixens kept chasing him across the tableau of his dreams, gaily shouting all manner of illegal, immoral, and illicit promises after him while they tried to subdue him with countless yards of flowered yellow calico.

Chapter Six

It was one of those cool, crisp mornings when the very air seemed packed with vitality-giving qualities and the heavy dew on the grass and bushes sparkled like precious stones in the bright sunlight. Faro had risen at the first bugler's call, jostled his way through the crowds at the bathhouse, and gobbled a hurried breakfast at the enlisted men's mess hall. By the time the orderly arrived at seven with the news that the buggy was hitched and Marantha Volney was ready to leave, he was shaved, brushed, shined, and ready to walk out the door.

Marantha was waiting for him over by the stables, all smiles and looking just about as good as any woman had a right to. She was wearing an emerald-green satin dress which buttoned high up the front to her neck, fitting her upper body like a coat of paint and flaring out in the skirts with great pleated waves of petticoats.

They drove out the east gate of the fort and took a

left, heading north toward the Mako River Road which traversed the seventy or so miles from Timberline to the river's end at Mako Lake. Once they had turned left again, they were on the main road heading west toward town. From the first moment that they passed out of sight of the fort, Marantha had scooted over close beside him, her body tight against him from knee to shoulder and both their sets of legs smothered beneath the blanket of her skirts. It was for warmth, she explained, but staying warm was not the only reaction he felt to her nearness and the subtle, delightful pressure of her pliant breast against his upper arm. It seemed as if a pleasant, tingling expectancy had permeated his whole nervous system.

At one point Faro stopped the buggy briefly to fold the top back so the sun could warm their backs, and it was then that he first noticed the neatly wrapped and tied bundle tucked down behind the seat.

"What's this?" he asked, poking the bundle with his finger.

"Well, I couldn't hardly come back from town without my yellow calico, could I?" Marantha asked with a bright smile. "Actually, Mrs. Filpot sold me several yards of what she had bought when she stopped by the fort on her way home, but I'm glad now that I never took it out and showed it to Nehemiah." Faro just grinned as he stepped back up into the carriage and clicked the horse into motion.

He let the horse set its own leisurely pace, and soon they were moving along at scarcely more than a snail's crawl, which was quite all right with both of them. They were in no hurry to get anywhere, and he thought that the only thing which would truly surprise him was if they ever actually did reach town today. For his part, he couldn't care less if he ever laid eyes on the face of another banker again, and he thought Marantha showed no strong indications that she wanted to pass the morning rummaging through the wares of a dry-goods store.

After about the first hour they had passed no more than two miles from the fort when Marantha said suddenly, "Turn here, Faro. I want to show you something."

It took him a moment to figure out where "here" was, but then he spotted it, an overgrown wagon trail leading off on a meandering route into the thick forest south of them. It took them some time to pass through the region of ordinary pines and firs, but at last they entered yet another grove of the awesome giant red-wood trees which dotted this entire part of the state. Finally, in the midst of the grove, she motioned off to the right, away from the faint trail they were following.

"It's about a quarter mile over there," she said. "The ground here is flat and clear, so the horse and buggy shouldn't have any problem making it."

As he had seen happen before with Nye, Marantha's whole tone and mood changed in the midst of these titans. She seemed awestruck and subdued, and Faro felt as if he could feel some sort of charge of energy radiating from her as she gazed about in wonderment.

"Sometimes I dream about these trees," she said quietly. "They're so straight and long and solid, so ... I don't know quite how to express it ... so ..."

"Phallic?" Faro prompted.

Marantha turned to him, her mouth open in surprise and slight embarrassment. "How did you guess?" she asked.

"Just a long shot." He chuckled.

"It's probably about the craziest thing you've ever heard," she said, "dreaming about doing it with trees, especially ones as big and as old as these are."

"There ain't no accounting for what we come up

with in our dreams," Faro said. "But, hell, I figure it's the same for everybody. What we can't have or can't get away with or wish we could do in real life, we take care of with our wild imaginations in our sleep. If you want to dream about making it with trees, that's your business."

Who was he to judge a woman who dreamed about screwing trees? Faro thought. The things that had gone on last night after those redheaded she-animals finally caught up to him couldn't exactly be classified as your everyday occurrences, either.

Marantha did not even have to tell Faro when they reached the spot she wanted him to see. As soon as the great fallen redwood log came into view, he knew that this had been their objective. At its base end the tree was more than twenty feet high, and the remainder of it stretched out through the forest like a freight train. Faro stopped the buggy near the tangle of rotting roots at one end, and both of them stepped to the ground.

"But this isn't all there is to see," Marantha told him with sudden, girlish enthusiasm. "Come on!"

She took his hand and led him into the midst of the roots, and after ducking beneath one low overhang Faro saw what she was so thrilled about. The center of the tree had rotted away, leaving a shaft about eight feet in diameter and six feet off the ground right down the heart of the giant. And closer by, someone had hacked a winding set of steps out of the roots, so that it was possible to walk right up into the redwood.

Marantha hiked her skirts up above her knees to keep them out of the way, then scampered up the steps and disappeared from view. "Come on, Faro," she urged him, her voice echoing dully from inside.

After he had mounted the steps, it took his eyes a

moment to adjust to the dim light of the chamber he found himself in, but slowly the features of the place began to emerge.

"Some time or other," Marantha told him, "someone actually lived in here. Look. Here's where they carried in rocks to build their fire on, and over there is where they carved out shelves to keep their food and things on. And see up there? They even carved long narrow slits to let light in."

It was a truly incredible sight, finding such a well-organized home right here in the heart of a fallen tree. And Faro knew that the former occupant of this place could have been someone who had gone away only months before, or some Indian who had died two or three hundred years ago. Redwood decayed very slowly, and it undoubtedly took centuries for one of these monsters to rot away.

"How in the world did you ever find this place?" Faro asked.

"I used to ride a lot back before the Indian trouble started," Marantha told him, "and this redwood grove was one of my favorite places to come. One day a thunderstorm blew up and I ducked in among those roots out there, hoping I could find some kind of shelter from the rain. That's when I saw the steps and came up here to explore. From time to time I bet I've imagined just about every detail of the way they kept house here, and I've decided it wasn't just one person who lived alone here. It must have been a man and a woman."

"I'd be obliged to know how you figured that one out," Faro said.

"By the bed!" she told him gaily. "Come on. I'll show you." She led him about thirty feet farther back into the tree to a point where the light was only a dim gray haze about them. There she stooped down and said, "You can't see it too well, but you can feel where they've carved out a slight depression for the hips and left another lump at the top to use as a pillow. And it's plenty wide enough for two people. Feel for yourself."

Faro knelt beside her and fumbled around obligingly. Sure enough, what with the inch-thick coating of soft moss which grew there, the place felt suitable for any of the purposes a bed might be used for.

"Seems like a bed, all right," Faro said. "Let's try 'er out and see if she works."

"That's precisely the purpose of this whole trip out here, my dear," Marantha told him throatily. "I know it works for sleeping, for I've taken naps here alone, but as far as other things are concerned . . ."

"Well, there's no way of knowing except by doing," Faro told her enthusiastically.

As they wrestled hurriedly out of their clothes Faro's only regret was that he would not be able to witness the spectacle of her dynamic body as it emerged from her clothing. That was a sight that he would have loved to see for the first time in bright sunlight, where he could study every curve and detail of her lovely form. But he did have to admit that their dim, damp surroundings seemed to add a sort of illicit sensuality to the occasion. And the slight coolness in the air made the experience all the more enjoyable when they lay down and their warm, naked bodies came together at last.

Marantha was breathing huskily and her heart was racing like a steam engine as their bodies pressed tightly together and they kissed for the first time. She plunged her tongue hungrily into his mouth as if she might be searching for a four-course dinner in there, and her nails stabbed sharply into the hard flesh of his shoulders as his finger raked thrillingly down her spine to the two firm mounds of her hips.

"That gives me chills that zip right down my back-bone to you-know-where." She shivered. "I can't hardly stand it, but if you stop, I'll strangle you!"

Faro accommodatingly worked the chills for all they were worth, all the while feeling her churning frenzy increase to the point where she seemed to become a quivering, writhing mass of flesh in his arms. It was as if a sort of frantic aspect had overtaken their joining, and he was not really sure what he had done that was so thrilling as to put her in this sort of state. But here he was, grappling and wrestling with a wild woman if there ever was one.

At last she rolled him roughly over onto his back and pounced on him like a she-lion springing for the kill. With no semblance of gentleness, she impaled herself on his rigid, waiting member, cut loose with a howl that might well have been heard clear back at the fort had they been outside, and collapsed forward onto him like a bundle of wet laundry. Then she lay for a while, quivering involuntarily as spasm after spasm racked her innards.

"Hellfire," Faro exclaimed in wonderment. "You mean you've done got yours already?"

"Ummm-hummm," she moaned, her face muffled against his chest.

"Then I'd say you must have needed it something fierce," he observed.

"I've been needing a good fucking for a long time," Marantha told him breathlessly, "and the second I laid eyes on you in the washhouse yesterday, I had the feeling that you were the man I was going to get it from."

"Well, what with you being a married woman and all," he said, "it seems like you wouldn't hardly never reach such a point of desperation."

"I've got me a piece of broom handle that I slick

down with mineral oil and use sometimes," Marantha revealed quietly. "And other times I wait up late until Nehemiah comes in from work and do my best to get him worked up and in the proper spirit of things. But after eight years of marriage to a man that's married to the army, it seems more and more like the two recourses I have are not that much different from one another, and neither one of them even comes close to the kind of satisfaction I need."

"Well, ma'am," Faro promised her, "I'll be most gratified to do all I can for you and see if that don't suffice to your needs a slight bit better than a broom handle."

He was intensely, almost painfully, aware that his member was still rigid and ready inside her. And though he had to admit that it wasn't any hardship just lying here with his personals closely enveloped in the warm sac of her womanhood, the idea did cross his mind how much better things would be if they began to bounce and jounce about a bit. That one hard plunge might have been enough to send steam shooting out of Marantha's ears on this particular occasion, but it was going to take a little more time and effort to do the same for him.

He rolled her over onto her back, careful not to slam her against the hard wood beneath them, and then began to arch in and out of her with smooth, rhythmic thrusts. She lay quite still beneath him for a while, enjoying the tranquility of this kind of intercourse after the violence of moments before. Faro dipped his head down beside hers and gently traced the shape of her muscles down across her neck and onto her shoulders, eliciting quiet coos of pleasure from her.

"See, there's this kind of fucking, too, slow and gentlelike," he murmured into her ear. "And damned if I don't think it's better a lot of the time. It's like climbing a mountain in easy stages till you finally reach the top. That other kind, it's like falling off the mountain."

"I don't mind the fall"—Marantha giggled—"just so long as I land on the right piece of equipment in the end."

Despite her climax of only a few minutes before, it soon became apparent that she was building up for another one, but this one promised to be of a much different nature. Faro first began to sense it by the delightful ripplings of the muscles inside her, and he found that it triggered an intense excitement within him to know that she was on the brink again. With great effort, he kept his pace steady until the last possible instant, then entered into the finale with a final few straight, hard thrusts.

Marantha signaled the onrush of pleasure this time by a series of low, throaty moans, rather than with a repeat of all the hollering she had done before. As her body trembled and arched repeatedly beneath him Faro felt the rush of hot juices leaving his body and braced himself for the moment of excruciating delight which followed.

This time he was the one transformed into a bundle of limp, wet rags, but Marantha did not complain as the full weight of his body descended onto her. She knew that at the moment he was spent, in no shape to exert even the effort it would take to roll to the side.

"Mmmm, mmmm, mmmm," she crooned from below him. "That was some good little bit better than a broom handle, or maybe even a fat, ripe cucumber."

Later they went back outside of the tree, still naked, and climbed up the tangle of roots until they reached the high, curved crest of the fallen tree. And there they sat for a long time, feeling elated and vastly superior to all they surveyed below them. Only the other titans of the forest still dwarfed them, but that was all right, for now they felt a sort of kinship with the massive redwoods. They had probed deep within the heart of one of their number, also probing each other in the bargain, and now it seemed almost as if they shared some sort of unexpressible ancient secret with these ageless giants.

"Thanks, Faro," Marantha murmured from where she lay close beside him atop the tree.

"What for?" he asked. "If any thanks were necessary, I figure they should be exchanged both ways, for we both got our equal measure of fun out of this day's doings."

Here at last he was finally able to take care of all the looking he hadn't had the opportunity to do in the dim light inside. Her face just now, outlined with the flaming red hair and in glowing repose after the satisfying intercourse, was a delightful picture to gaze at even by itself, but on down there was plenty more which drew his vision like a magnet. Even lying flat on her back, her creamy breasts arched up from her chests like half-moons, or perhaps more appropriately like twin scoops of vanilla ice cream, each tipped with a sweet brown cherry. Her flat, smooth belly seemed to stretch on practically forever before finally being interrupted by the curvature of her pelvic bones and swooping down at last to a vortex of curly, reddish-brown hair. Her legs were long and sleek, a harmonious blend of gentle, alluring curves melting into one another.

But despite the idyllic circumstances, reality was still out there waiting to pounce. The peace and perfection of the moment ended suddenly and unexpectedly like a swift kick from a steel-toed boot when Marantha asked, "Where will we go when we leave here, darling?"

He knew what she meant, though he tried desperately to make it seem otherwise. "Er, uh, back to the fort, I reckon," he stammered. "When it gets on toward noon, that husband of yours will be looking for you, and what with him being the honcho of upward of three hundred armed men, I don't think I'd like to be the one to stir up no suspicions in his mind by delivering you back late."

"Silly, I know we have to go back to the fort when we leave this particular spot," Marantha told him. "But I'm talking about later. What would happen if I decided to go with you when you left Fort Volney and Timberline and this whole part of the state?"

I'd shit like a coon eating green persimmons, Faro thought. That's what would happen. But, of course, such a response was not appropriate for the occasion. "It's an interesting thought," he told her.

"Interesting?" Marantha responded. "After what went on inside there, seeing how well we fit together and all, I thought the prospect would delight you, Faro."

"Oh, well, it does, ma'am. I'm delighted as hell, but . . ." It wouldn't do to piss her off at this juncture, he knew, nor to let her know yet what a cockeyed pack of schoolgirl nonsense he thought her suggestion was. Many a willing and eager damsel had turned an honest, well-intended screwing into a rape after time and her temper went to work on the subject.

"It's love, Faro," Marantha told him sincerely. "There's not one single doubt about it in my mind. This whole day has just been one wonderful, uninterrupted fantasy for me. Escaping Nehemiah and that dreary prison I live in, making love there inside the tree where I'd lain so many times wishing it could happen. Even now it's still going on, being out here stark naked like nature's children, sharing our secret love with the wilderness and the open spaces. Oh, Faro, I want you again, right now, right here on top of this tree!"

"Now, hold on, Marantha!" he told her. "Just wait a minute. I figure we'd better get this thing worked out and settled amongst ourselves before we go on to any other kinds of pastimes." She rolled on her side and reached out to gently grip his penis, making it difficult to keep his concentration. But he plunged on, doing the best he could.

"See, ma'am, I myself am a gambling man by choice and by profession, and that line of work just naturally necessitates a good deal of steady travel. Hell, it ain't hardly ever that I settle in one place for more than a few weeks at a time, and when I do stop, most of my time is spent in smoky saloons, rowdy gambling dens, and risky hellholes. It's positively no life for any kind of lady, leastwise not one with your class and promise."

"But I'm hungry to travel around like that and see something of the country while I'm still young enough to enjoy it fully," Marantha pleaded. "Up until I was twenty-two, I lived all my life on a farm eleven miles out of South Platte, Nebraska. Then, when Nehemiah Volney came along and asked me to marry him, he promised me he would take me away to a better life. But in eight years of marriage we've lived on six different army posts. The longest we've ever been anywhere is here at Fort Volney, and look where it's at, for heaven's sake.

"Faro, if you think I'd squawk about always moving from one city to the next, leading the kind of life you want, you're wrong. It all sounds terribly exciting, and I know I'd love it!" Faro just sat staring at her, no longer knowing what to make of any of it. "Aren't there some successful women in your profession?" she asked.

"A few know their stuff well enough to do right good at it," Faro allowed. "I hear tell that the likes of Minnie the Gambler and Poker Alice have done all right for themselves in the business, but others I know of have had to turn to another, more personal sort of game to make their way. There ain't no guarantees."

"I'd take my chances, darling," Marantha assured him. "And one good year spent with a man like you would be worth eight more living with a man like Nehemiah in places like Fort Volney. Take me, Faro. Please say you'll take me along when you leave!"

Faro studied her features for a long, serious moment before finally telling her, "Okay. We'll leave together when I go. But I have to have one promise from you. Swear you won't do anything nor say anything that would give your husband the slightest suspicion of this. If he even got a hint that we had cooked up something like this between us, he'd have me skinned out alive and strung up for buzzard bait before you could say ace high."

"I do so promise, Faro," she told him solemnly. "I'll be so sweet to him he'll think a little piece of heaven chipped off and dropped right down in the same house with him."

"That's fine," Faro told her with a grin. "You treat him like some kind of teddy bear so he won't have any suspicions . . ."

". . . right up to the time we sneak away together," Marantha interrupted with a grin.

"Right up to then," Faro said.

All during the ride back to the fort, Marantha was like a tub of butter melted and poured all over him. She spent much of the time with her face buried in his lap, giving him a taste of what delights were in store for him when they made their break together.

But Faro did not, could not, devote his full attention to what might otherwise be quite an entertaining way to pass the time during a long buggy ride. Part of his mind was trying to decide whether he had been an utter lunatic to make such a wild promise to this woman, or whether, as it had seemed at the time, there was no other way out of the predicament.

Scenario after scenario kept flashing through his mind.

In one he had told Marantha Volney that he would not take her anywhere, and soon after arriving back at the fort, she had gone running for her husband, screaming rape at the top of her lungs.

In another, she could not resist the temptation to taunt the major with her imminent departure, and in a fit of frenzy he had beaten out of her the name of the man she planned to make her escape with.

And finally he pictured the two of them fleeing the fort in the dead of night, riding as if the devil were on their tails but not quite making it beyond the range of Nehemiah Volney's vengeance.

And always the imagined scenes ended in roughly the same manner—there was blood all around, his; plenty of ear-piercing screams, his, too; and a glimpse of sliced-off pecker being ground into the dirt by the hard heel of a military boot. Guess whose!

Thank you, ma'am, for a very fine morning inside the belly of a stately redwood tree, he thought, but no, thanks, to all the rest. . . .

Chapter Seven

When they were within about half a mile of the fort, Marantha asked Faro to stop the buggy so she could go down to the edge of the river to refresh herself and get her clothing and hair in order before they got back. Faro thought it was a good idea; it wouldn't do at all for her to return with flecks and bits of moss still clinging to her dress and petticoats and with her hair all awry.

He pulled the buggy off the road into a small grove of trees, then walked partway with her down the sloping bank to the edge of the water. In a lush grassy area she stripped off her dress, petticoats, and shoes, and then, wearing only her white cotton camisole, she waded out into the edge of the river to splash water onto her face, arms and legs.

"Ooh! It's cold!" she exclaimed with a tinkling, girlish giggle from where she stood about fifty feet away. "But it feels good, too."

She stayed in the water only a moment, then returned to her clothes and dried herself off with one of the petticoats before shaking her clothes out and beginning to dress again.

For a moment Faro idly turned his eyes away from Marantha and glanced away to the opposite side of the river fifty yards away. The bank there was covered with a thick tangle of brush and scrub trees, and farther away was a wide belt of tall pine trees.

At first Faro hardly noticed the flicker of movement in the brush on the far side of the water. This area was well populated with birds and small game of all varieties, and here at the water's edge their numbers could be expected to be especially thick. But then, when a bush wiggled more noticeably, Faro concentrated his attention on it, and he was sure he could faintly make out the form of some living thing there that was much larger than any jackrabbit or raccoon. Was it just his imagination, or was that really the outline of a man's face and shoulders?

Slowly, as if nothing of interest had caught his attention, he turned his head back toward Marantha, but he kept his eyes cocked off to the side toward the spot where the movement had occurred. In a moment, as they eased back through the brush away from the water, Faro finally caught a glimpse of them—three brown forms, all with round, flat faces and long black hair, and wearing no sort of clothing from the waist up.

As Marantha started back toward him, dressed now and combing her fingers back across her hair to smooth it down, Faro decided to say nothing to her about seeing the three men in the bushes. It would only scare her and not get them back to the haven of Fort Volney any quicker.

"How do I look?" she asked brightly as she accepted Faro's hand and stepped up into the waiting buggy.

"Gorgeous, of course," Faro told her. "If you looked any better, I don't think I could stand it."

"No, silly." She giggled, obviously delighted by the compliment. "I mean, do I look like a lady that's just finished doing what we've just finished doing?"

"Well, that twinkle in your eye might tend to give you away," Faro told her with a grin, "but if you're referring to the condition of your clothes and suchlike, I'd say you look just as pert and tidy as the minute we drove out the gates of the fort early this morning."

As soon as they were settled on the carriage seat, Faro clicked the horse into motion and urged it to a trot. He was in a hurry to get back to the fort now, not only to return the major's wife at the expected hour but also to report the sighting of the three mysterious men in the bushes. Surely, with Volney's passion for such tidbits of intelligence, that would gain Faro several points in the commander's book.

Once they reached the fort, Faro deposited Marantha Volney at her front step and returned the buggy to the stables, then hurried across the parade grounds to the headquarters building. But once he was inside the orderly room, the clerk there told him that the major was tied up and could not be disturbed.

"But I've got some information about the Indians that he needs to hear," Faro protested.

"That's the same thing he's getting right now," the clerk informed him. "Some old geezer come in here about fifteen minutes ago, babbling something about warpaths and wholesale slaughter, and the major and Mr. Ashford are in there trying to get his story sorted out."

"Well, hell!" Faro grumbled in disgust, dropping down into one of the chairs in the orderly room. Here he finally had his first chance to deliver some concrete information and join the ranks of the good guys in

Major Volney's eyes, and suddenly the opportunity had been snatched right out from under him. What would the commander care for his measly little yarn about seeing three men slink through some bushes, when at almost the same time he had an honest-to-goodness massacre to worry and fret over?

He had to wait another quarter hour before the door to Volney's office opened and Jason Ashford came out, accompanied by the apparent bearer of this most recent piece of grisly tidings.

Faro joined them as they went outside, and Ashford paused on the steps of the headquarters to introduce Faro to the man with him, Ab Eisentier.

"Ab's just come with the news about how the Leatherfoot seem to have attacked the settlement at Crystal Creek and killed everyone there," Ashford said.

"Warn't no seemin' to it, boy," Eisentier proclaimed with a note of irritation in his voice. "Man 'n' boy, I been trompin' these here Sierries for nigh onto fifty of my sixty-eight years, an' I seen me some gawd-awful things in that time. But never in all my born days have I ever seen nothin' that could compare to this!"

Eisentier was a tall man with shoulders only slightly bowed by his advanced age. The shaggy wilderness of white hair on his head and his unkept mass of gray beard seemed on the verge of engulfing his entire face, leaving only one broad strip of heavily tanned flesh exposed in the vicinity of his nose and eyes. No trace of his mouth was visible through the undergrowth, and the bushy beard on his chin bobbed almost comically with his hurried, excited revelations.

"He says he counted fifteen to twenty bodies of white settlers out there," Ashford said.

"Pieces of 'em, I said," Eisentier corrected him, "Jes' dad-blamed pieces of 'em, scattered every which away. It was horrible, plumb horrible."

"All right, Ab," Ashford told the grizzled old mountain man. "You cart yourself on over to the mess hall yonder and tell the cook I said to fix you up with whatever you want to eat. Remember, the major said he wants to have the troops mustered and mounted in two hours, ready to ride out for Crystal Creek."

Faro waited until Eisentier was out of earshot, then turned to Ashford and asked, "What about his story, Jason? From what you've told me of the Leatherfeet, mayhem and wholesale slaughter don't sound much like the kind of tactics they'd be inclined to use."

"They don't, for a fact," Ashford said, shaking his head in puzzlement. "There's several pretty big holes in the old man's yarn, and that's only one of them. Besides that, the Crystal Creek settlement is west of Mako Lake, far out of the district that the Leatherfoot last called their own. If they were going to slaughter anybody, which I wouldn't hardly expect of them in the first place, it seems like it would be some of the newcomers to the north of the lake that moved in and grabbed that territory the minute the Indians vacated it.

"I just don't know what to make of this," the scout admitted. "There wasn't any doubt in my mind that the old man had been through Crystal Creek some time or another, because he knew the lay of the buildings and suchlike. But that doesn't necessarily mean he stumbled through there at just the right time to see bodies scattered around like cordwood."

"I guess there's no need to ask what the major's reaction was," Faro said.

"It was predictable," Ashford told him. "He's sent me out to round up his executive officer and all his company commanders for a council of war before they head out, and I don't see much need of trying to talk him out of it this time. Hell, for all I know, it's the right thing to do, but down in my gut I've got a rotten feeling about this whole thing. I can't quite explain it, but I've had the same kind of feeling enough times before to know not to ignore it completely."

"Well, with all this going on," Faro observed, "I guess when I get done throwing in my two cents' worth, it'll only serve to add to the confusion."

"How's that?" Ashford asked.

Quickly Faro told the scout about the three forms he had seen in the bushes, though he withheld the true reasons for the stop along the river.

"You'd better head on in and tell the major about it," Ashford said, "but I'm afraid it's going to be pretty small potatoes to him alongside this Crystal Creek thing."

"I figured as much myself," Faro agreed.

They parted in a moment, Ashford to round up the fort's officers and Faro to go in and report his sighting to the fort commander. When he was admitted into Volney's office, the major was busy honing his saber with a fine black whetstone.

"Come in, Blake. Come in," Volney said impatiently. "And whatever it is that you've got on your mind, make it quick. I've got a hundred details to take care of, and only a short time to do them in."

"I won't take a minute, Major," Faro said. "I just wanted to tell you about these Indians I saw on my way back from town."

"Indians?" Volney said, suddenly shifting his entire attention to Faro. "How many and where at?"

"Well, your wife and I stopped to water the horse at the river about half a mile west of here on the way back from town," Faro continued. "And I spotted them in the brush on the other side of the river. I only caught a glimpse of them, mind you, but there were three, I think, and it seemed to me that they must be Indians."

"Is that it, Blake?" Volney snapped at him impatiently. "Here I am with a full-scale massacre on my hands, and you're taking up my time with maybe having seen something that seemed like Indians. You sure you didn't just see a bush blowing in the wind and then let your imagination turn it into something else?"

"Well, Major," Faro growled back at him, "I've seen a group of bushes in my time, but never none with long black hair and bare brown chests like these had. But you make what you want out of it. If you say Injuns are bushes or bushes are Injuns, it don't make much difference to me."

"I don't know what you saw out there, Blake, and right now, frankly, I don't care," the major told him. "The only thing I've got on my mind at the moment is going out there to round up that pack of murdering redskins before they have time to butcher any more innocent white settlers. And I would appreciate it if you would kindly haul yourself out of here so I can get to that task forthwith."

"I'll be damned glad to oblige you in that," Faro said, turning and slamming the door behind him on the way out. Still burning inwardly from the shoddy treatment, he met Ashford in the middle of the parade grounds, and the two of them paused to talk again.

"Well, what'd he say?" Ashford asked.

"I'd just like to know how a thick-skulled jackass like him ever got put in charge of anything," Faro growled angrily. "He hasn't got brains enough to fill a good-sized thimble."

"I take it he wasn't exactly excited by the news you brought him," Ashford observed dryly.

"Not exactly, or even a little bit."

"Well, keep in mind that unavenged disasters look bad on reports back to the War Department," Ashford said. "And generals in Washington have about as much sympathy and understanding toward an officer that can't get the job done as a cougar has for a wounded fawn. Volney's fighting for his career here, and he damn well knows it."

"So a whole tribe of people has to suffer so he can gain a few more points toward making colonel," Faro said.

"Something like that."

In a moment Ashford started again toward the headquarters to take part in Volney's meeting, and Faro returned to the front of the barracks to take his familiar seat outside the door of Ashford's quarters. Some orders had apparently gone out, because across the parade grounds dozens of soldiers were already gathering at the stables to saddle their mounts. Over by the gates, crews of men were busy lowering the fort's small fieldpieces down from the walls with block and tackle and mounting them on wheeled carriages. Volney obviously planned to go all out on this one.

The meeting of the officers was a short one, and within a few minutes Faro saw Jason Ashford come out of the headquarters building and start over toward the barracks. Faro expected the scout to go inside and immediately collect his gear to depart, but instead Ashford took a seat outside and began watching the preparations just as Faro was.

"Aren't you going with them?" Faro asked.

"Nope. I'm taking a pass on this one," Ashford said. "At first Volney wouldn't hear of me staying behind, but what with most of the command gone for the devil knows how long, I pointed out to him that it wouldn't hurt to leave at least one experienced Indian fighter behind, just in case. Hell, the lieutenant he talked about leaving back here is such a youngster that he don't even shave except about every third day. They have that old geezer Ab Eisentier to guide them, so they don't need me."

"How many men is he leaving behind?" Faro asked.

"Two squads, about thirty men," Ashford said. "I convinced him that he shouldn't just leave this place absolutely defenseless, just in case them boogeybears you saw in the bushes did actually prove out to be flesh-and-blood Indians."

"They were real, all right," Faro assured him, "though I don't have no notion what it means, them being seen this close to the fort. Under the circumstances, it seems to me like this is the last place they would want to be."

"Well, they're probably just scouts sent out to keep an eye on what we're doing, but, like I said before, there ain't no predicting what this new mystery man, Chief Burning Wind, might be up to."

Within three quarters of an hour, all of the two hundred seventy men who were to ride out on the campaign were assembled in two long mounted rows which stretched from the front gates of the fort nearly to the back wall. Volney, mounted on a spirited sorrel, made a brief inspection from one end of the long formation to the other, then rode to the gates and gave the command to ride. Company commanders and then platoon sergeants relayed the message, and the men turned their horses in unison and started forward. At the rear of the column two supply wagons and the men pulling the artillery behind their horses fell in line.

"Man, that takes me back," Ashford observed as the column threaded its way out the gates of the compound. "There ain't nothing like the feeling a man gets when he's riding out with his outfit on a piece of business like this, feeling all tough and salty, like you and the men around you could lick any Indian nation ten times your size. But deep down inside you there's this little knot of fear, too, and you're wondering, 'Will I die this time, or is this the day that I finally can't take it anymore and turn yellow?' Faro, there ain't nothing like it!"

"I believe you," Faro said. He'd have to, because it was a sure bet that he didn't ever want to be a part of such goings-on himself. There were enough dangers which came up just in the natural course of things in his life and line of work without him ever having to go out and look for any extras.

As the last fieldpiece tumbled heavily out the entrance and two blue-clad soldiers swung the wide gates closed Ashford rose from his seat. "I guess I'd best hunt up that shavetail Volney left in charge here," he said, "and try to coach him in some of the ways and means of keeping body and soul together under dire circumstances. It might be a lesson he'll be glad he learned in the coming days and nights."

A mood of tense anticipation seemed to drift over the few remaining inhabitants of Fort Volney as nightfall descended. In the light of day no one acted particularly nervous or worried about the departure of the majority of the fort's defenders, but with the coming of darkness that attitude slowly changed. Unexplained shapes and shadows inside the fort's walls seemed to take on ominous human qualities, and the scant guards scattered out around the parapets listened closely to each sound in the blackness beyond, nervously wondering if it signaled the nearness of some hidden enemy.

For want of anything better to do after supper, Faro found Ashford and the young officer in charge, Lieutenant Beale, and joined them on a walking tour of the fort's defenses. Ashford and Beale had been together since Volney and the others had left, planning and discussing strategies and ensuring that every remaining man stayed constantly vigilant.

The three of them strolled across from the headquarters toward the gate and mounted the set of steps leading to the parapets about fifteen feet above. Then they began a tour of the walls, pausing occasionally so the lieutenant could give each of the scattered guards a few words of encouragement and caution.

The moon had not yet risen, and, gazing out into the blackness, Faro realized that a quiet Indian could conceivably advance to within a few yards of the walls of the fort without being detected. As a matter of fact, in some places where there were no guards they might even have a chance of scaling the walls and getting inside before anybody knew they were there.

In slow stages they worked their way along one wall after another until at last they found themselves completing the circle and approaching the last of the four log towers at the corners of the fort. The lone man on duty there turned expectantly, rifle still in hand, as the three men approached.

"That you, Lootenant?" the man asked in the darkness.

"It's me, Angus," Beale told him.

"What time you figure it is, sir?"

"Nine o'clock, maybe a quarter past," the lieutenant said.

"Is that all? Seems like I been up here so long I was sure half the night had done passed already. But hell! It ain't hardly even started."

"It'll be a long one for everybody," Beale told him. "But that's just the way it is. And tomorrow might be exactly the same, and the night after that, and the night after that . . ."

"That's just fucking dandy . . . sir," the trooper grumbled.

"Have you got your orders straight, Angus?" Ashford asked the soldier. "If anything starts, every man here has to know immediately what to do with himself."

"If I spot any redskins, I'm s'posed to stick here until I'm sure it's an all-out attack and not just a sortie," the soldier said. "If they storm the walls, I'm to hold as long as I can, then fall back to the headquarters building."

"That's right," Ashford said. "But if they hit the walls in some other spot, you move around and help the men there. In case they don't know how many men are left in here, we want to create the impression that the fort is still well protected. It might or might not discourage them from trying to breach the walls, but it's the only trump card we've got."

When their tour of the walls was completed, Ashford, the lieutenant, and Faro went back down the stairs to the ground and started across to the headquarters. They were only about halfway to their destination when a shot rang out suddenly and startlingly in the distance beyond the fort's wall.

"Over here!" someone shouted from high up along the south wall. "It come from over here!"

But before anybody could make a move to reinforce that side of the fort, other shots began sounding from all directions outside the walls, and a moment later Faro realized that the faint twacks which he kept hearing on the ground all around were arrows landing.

"Blake, you go find the major's wife and get her up to the headquarters in a hurry," Ashford shouted at Faro. "Me and the lieutenant are going up to check this situation out, but I suspect we'll be joining you there shortly."

As Faro turned and trotted off toward Volney's house the guards on the walls above were just beginning to return the Indians' fire. But Faro recognized that as a useless waste of ammunition. In this darkness, nobody was going to be able to see well enough to draw a clear bead on anyone else.

Marantha Volney was waiting for him as he burst through the front door of her house and urgently called out her name. She had all the lamps out, and as she fell against him, sobbing, her body trembled in his arms and he could feel the moisture of her tears as her face burrowed against his neck.

"Oh, Faro darling," she whimpered. "I knew you would come for me. I was sure you would risk your life to save mine."

"Ashford sent me over to get you," he said, still breathing hard from his sprint across the parade grounds. "Come on. We're going over to hole up in the headquarters building."

"I'll just get some clothes from the bedroom before we go," she said. "I was already dressed for bed."

"You could die worrying about what to put on," Faro told her. "I suggest we get over there first, and then worry about what might be showing later."

Taking her by the hand, he tugged her out the front door and started away, but almost immediately she stumbled and fell to the ground.

"I'm barefooted," she pleaded with him, "and I stepped on something."

"Well, hell!" Faro exclaimed in irritation. In an instant he had scooped her up in his arms and was on his way again at top speed. A half-dozen soldiers had already congregated in the orderly room as Faro rushed in, but they hardly had time to catch a startled glimpse of his half-dressed burden before he hustled her across the room and deposited her in her husband's office.

After closing the door and firing up a lamp to a low flickering glow, he turned and caught his first glimpse of her revealing costume. The nightgown she was wearing looked more like a pale, mint-green pall of smoke around her than any sort of clothing, and beneath it her body was visible in intoxicating detail.

"I put this on because I was sure you'd find some way to come and see me tonight," she told him.

Faro had to admit that the thought had crossed his mind. With Volney and most of the garrison away from the fort, it would be no great chore to slip in for an enjoyable interlude in Marantha's arms. But the notion had never gotten beyond the planning stage.

"Get under something and stay clear of the window," he told her urgently. "I'll come back and check on you when I can."

He was halfway to the door before Marantha called out to try to stop him. "Wait, Faro!" she said. "Are you going to just leave me here by myself? I'm terrified."

"You ain't the only one in that condition, lady," he assured her. "But there's not a damn thing I can do about it right now."

"You could stay here and just hold me, darling. Then I wouldn't be so afraid."

"Wal, I kind of thought I might be more use helping fight off this attack," he snapped at her with rising irritation. "Now, you stay put and do what I told you. And cut out that darling stuff, too. It's just not the time for it."

He closed the door on her sobbing and turned to watch the soldiers dash periodically inside the building in twos and threes. In a moment Lieutenant Beale came in and began dispersing the soldiers to various windows and entrances on both the first and second floors. At one point he started to send two men in to guard the window inside Major Volney's office, but Faro stopped them.

"The major's wife is in there, and in her hurry to get over here, she didn't exactly have time to . . . well, she's just not dressed decent quite yet. Let her be 'til I can round her up something more fitting to put on." Beale agreed with the wisdom of that suggestion and sent the two men off in another direction.

Jason Ashford was the last man to race inside, and once he was clear of the door, one of the troopers slammed it shut and dropped the heavy bar in place across it.

"Anybody take a head count yet?" Ashford asked the lieutenant. "Do we have any men missing?"

"Counting you and Mr. Blake here," the lieutenant said, "that makes thirty-two in all. We were lucky. We didn't lose a single man."

"Well, let's just hope the luck holds out," Ashford said. "It's hard to tell in the dark and all, but I'd put their strength at about sixty or seventy, but there may be more. Time I reached the door, a handful of them were already over the wall and were commencing to work on opening the gates."

"I've got men on all the doors and windows," Beale said. "Can you think of anything else we can do, Mr. Ashford?"

"We can wait," Ashford told him solemnly, "and hope that none of them Indians out there has a taste for whopping big bonfires."

Faro was about to find himself a place to sit down when the door to Major Volney's office opened a crack and Marantha peeked out timidly. Immediately the room began to grow quiet and soon everyone's eyes were drawn in her direction as if by a magnet. Only her face and a portion of her shoulder, covered with the silky, transparent green material, were in view.

"Mrs. Volney, are you all right?" Lieutenant Beale asked her.

"I want to see Mr. Blake for a moment," she said quietly.

Faro had been trying his best to ignore her but found it impossible. "Sorry," he mumbled to her. "I'll find you something to put on right away. It slipped my mind."

"You know that doesn't matter," she said more impatiently. "I want you to come in here *right now!*"

There was a faint note of hysteria in her voice which made Faro quick to comply with her summons. With all these men watching the two of them with puzzled interest, going in there while she was still so scantily dressed was the last thing he wanted to do, but there was no telling what kind of ruckus she might raise if he didn't.

He was already taking off his suit coat as he started across the room toward the door, explaining to nobody in particular and everybody in general, "She's so scared she don't know which way is up. I'll just give her my coat to wear so things'll be respectable enough."

As soon as he was in the office and the door was closed, Maratha advanced on him, fawning and groping, but Faro stopped her with a hand on one of her shoulders. "There's a time and a place for that sort of goings-on," he hissed at her in a harsh whisper, "and this ain't neither of the two!"

"I just felt like I had to have you hold me just for a little while," she said. "With all those Indians outside and such danger all around, this might be our last chance ever." She tried again to put her arms around him, but he still wouldn't permit it.

"If any of those men out there was to come in here and see us snuggled up belly to belly like that," he cautioned, "why, I'd be one gone gosling five minutes after your husband got back here to the fort. Now, you put on this damn coat, woman, and you start behaving yourself like a married woman ought to!"

Pouting, Marantha docilely allowed Faro to slip his jacket onto her and button up the three buttons in front. On her smaller frame it came all the way down to the middle of her thighs and provided her with at least a semblance of decent attire.

"But do you still love me?" she asked meekly. "Are we still going away together?"

"Nothing's changed from the way it was the other day," he assured her. "But if you keep up like you've been doing, there could be one hellacious change right around the corner. Your husband could change the state of my health from good, the way it is now, to plumb miserable."

"All right, I'll be good," Marantha promised, unexpectedly flashing him one of those fantastic smiles. "But you'll have to give me one kiss to seal the bargain."

Faro obliged her with a warm kiss, then gave her a pat on the rear end for good measure and said, "Lieutenant Beale wants to put some men in here to keep a watch out that window there. Is that all right?"

"Of course, if that's what you want," she said.

Within a few minutes Faro had brought in two soldiers to guard the window, and he had Marantha situated off to the far side of the room with Volney's large desk between her and the window to protect her from any stray bullets.

Chapter Eight

For a while everything was quiet outside the two-story log building, as if the Indians had crept off in silence once they had gained entrance to the fort. But inside the headquarters building, the besieged occupants believed that it must be a false calm before the Indians regrouped and planned the next step of their attack. Surely, they thought, the Indians outside would not withdraw and leave them alone after gaining so much ground so easily.

But, as minutes passed, no attack came. After the first hour of the wait, the moon began to rise above the treetops to the east, and with the pale illumination it provided, the men at the windows began to catch occasional glimpses of dark, silent forms moving around the interior of the fort. They stayed well away from the headquarters, however, and showed no signs of wanting to attack. Acting on a hunch, Ashford told the men not to fire, even if they had a clear shot, unless the Indians themselves resumed the fight. Hopes for survival began to blossom among the suddenly optimistic soldiers.

As more time passed, Lieutenant Beale eventually told some of the men that they could sleep at their assigned posts while others remained on guard. Faro found himself an out-of-the-way corner of the orderly room and curled up to try to rest. It was a chore, what with all the excitement and confusion of the place, but eventually he drifted off into a restless slumber.

Faro woke some indeterminate time later as a soldier shouted from across the room, "Lieutenant, sir, they're taking the dad-blamed horses!" Beale was not in the room, but an instant later he came thumping down the stairs from the second floor.

Soon they all began to hear the telltale clatter of horses' hooves, and all the men in the room crowded around the windows to watch helplessly as their horses were driven across the parade grounds and out the open gates of the fort.

"Volney's sure going to have my tail on the carpet over this," Beale mourned quietly. "I wouldn't be surprised if I lost my commission after tonight."

"I wouldn't sweat it," Ashford told him calmly. "Look at it this way. In the dark and outnumbered the way we are, it could have become a massacre, but you didn't lose a man all night. We can always replace horses a lot easier than we could the men who ride them.

"And besides, consider this," the scout went on. "Up until now, every time anybody's laid eyes on any of the Leatherfeet, they've always been on foot, and trying to track an Indian who's afoot is like trying to hang on to a handful of smoke. But horses leave a clear trail that can't be covered up so easily. All in all, I'd say these Indians made their first big mistake tonight by taking our mounts, and if they ride them to the place where their womenfolk and papooses are hidden, that'll be their second."

"You make it sound damn near like we've done the major a favor by letting these hostiles take the fort," Beale said with a note of skepticism in his voice.

They waited a reasonable time, but none of the soldiers spotted any more Indians slipping around the interior of the fort. Finally Ashford took a couple of men with him and slipped out to investigate. He returned a short time later with the news that the gates were closed again and all the Indians were gone.

Further investigation revealed that the Leatherfeet had taken not only the horses but also a number of rifles, some ammunition, and a good portion of the fort's supply of food staples. Just as dawn was breaking in the eastern sky, the lieutenant stationed a few of his men at strategic spots around the fort's walls, then sent the rest off to their barracks to rest. One young soldier, known for his fast running, was sent off toward town with orders to round up as many available horses as possible and bring them back to the fort.

Faro escorted Marantha Volney back to her house, refusing all the way her renewed demands for his loving attentions. The situation with her, Faro decided, was reaching the critical point, but he still had no idea how to deal with it. The best solution, of course, would be to just leave, but that was even more impossible now than it had been before. His horse had been taken with all the others, and he did not relish the idea of wandering around the countryside afoot, not with a pack of mounted, well-armed, and obviously aggressive Indians on the loose somewhere in the vicinity. Besides all that, he had his doubts about the warmth of the reception he might now receive in Timberline. Hobart

Nye was most likely planning some sort of vengeance for his mock hanging, and in addition Henry Sorbitt might also have figured out by now that his roulette wheel was gimmicked and have some pretty strong ideas about who had done it. There would be no refuge for him in the nearby town.

Faro returned to Ashford's quarters and plopped down tiredly on the cot he used there, but he slept only restlessly, plagued by thoughts of the many problems and difficulties which seemed to be festering all around him.

As soon as the fleet-footed trooper returned from town with fresh mounts, a courier was dispatched to carry word of the attack to Major Volney. Now, even more than before, Ashford believed that the major was out on a useless mission to Crystal Creek, and he speculated that when he got there, he would find the residents of the settlement whole and healthy. Ab Eisentier, the scout suspected, had picked up the threads of some garbled rumor somewhere during his travels and had hurried to the fort with it, craving the distinction of bearing important news.

That seemed to be the case when Volney and his men returned to the fort two days later. The settlers at Crystal Creek had been as surprised to see such a large contingent of soldiers arriving as the soldiers had been to find no evidence of carnage and destruction. The settlers were frightened enough, all right, but there had been no concrete sightings of any Indians lurking about, let alone any outright attacks. Not unexpectedly, old Ab Eisentier had slipped away in the night shortly after their arrival at Crystal Creek.

But as humiliating as the whole thing had been for Volney and his men, it did seem to have one positive result. Chastened by his own poor judgment, the major

was much more receptive to the sound advice Jason
Ashford offered. The scout's suggestion was that he
leave the fort with only a dozen handpicked men, following the trail of the Indians who had attacked them.
Then, when they located Burning Wind and his band,
word would be sent back and Volney could follow with
his full command.

Volney readily consented to the plan, not wanting
to risk having his fort captured again while he was
away. Such things looked bad in reports to the War
Department.

After a careful consideration of all the ifs, ands, and
possibilities, Faro reluctantly volunteered to accompany
Ashford on his scouting mission. Despite her assur-
ances, he had no confidence that Marantha Volney
could control the reckless abandon with which she had
been pursuing him, and his imagination painted a
grisly picture of him being tied to the mouth of a
loaded cannon with a grinning, maniacal Major Volney
ready to pull the lanyard. With any luck, he could peel
away from Ashford's bunch somewhere to the east and
head toward the nearest town with stage service north.
The time had come, he was absolutely convinced, to
continue his journey toward Seattle.

Within hours after Major Volney's return, Ashford
and his small band were on their way, riding northeast
in the general direction the Indians had taken two days
before. It was late afternoon already, but the scout
hoped to make a few miles before nightfall put a halt
to their travel. With him were Faro Blake, Lieutenant
Beale, and ten enlisted men, all carrying one week's
rations in packs behind their horses' saddles.

They soon reached the river and crossed it at the
same place the Indians had ridden their stolen horses
across. It was the best ford in the area, and the mud
along the banks still bore the unmistakable prints of

shod hooves. Up until now, at least, the Leatherfeet seemed to be making no attempt to hide their trail.

Ashford was in a better mood than Faro had seen him in for days, and he confided to Faro that, rather than sending for the troops and instigating an all-out battle when he found Burning Wind's band, he hoped to mediate a peaceful settlement of the conflict.

"We've been lucky so far," Ashford said. "Neither side has done anything that can't be undone yet. Granted they took a few horses and several stands of small arms, but those could be returned under the right conditions. The main thing is that no lives have been lost that we know about. Killing is the one thing that would set us all on an irreversible course to disaster."

"What makes you think they'll negotiate?" Faro asked.

"All that I've heard about Burning Wind makes me think so," the scout said. "If he's the great leader everybody says, then he must have the good sense to know that, with what little remains of his tribe, he has no chance of winning a war against the army. And if he had wanted to stir up a fight, he certainly had a chance the other night at the fort. But they just took what they wanted and didn't try to hurt anyone there. Think about it, Blake."

Faro did, and it made sense.

For some time he had not seen any sign of the path of the stolen horses, and soon he noticed that Ashford was no longer even making a show of studying the ground before them. Faro pondered that awhile, then finally figured out why.

"You know where they're at, don't you?" Faro asked Ashford quietly.

The scout cast a wry grin in Faro's direction and said, "I'm damn near positive I do. I've had my suspicions for a while, and then this afternoon, when this trail made a beeline in one direction, it made me sure. Have you ever wondered where the Leatherfoot Indians got their name?"

"What's that got to do with anything?" Faro asked.

"Well, have you?"

Faro allowed as how he had not.

"Well, they got their name after the tough hide on the soles of their feet that allowed them to walk bare-footed across the jagged lava beds up northeast of here. Tribal legend has it that for centuries, anytime they were threatened from any sort of outside invasion, they could always find safe haven there.

"This particular patch of lava is about two miles long and a mile wide at its widest point. Sometime back before history began, a volcano spewed melted rock up out of the ground and formed it. It's the most twisted combooberation of winding ravines, twisting trails, pits, and caves you ever saw, and the kind of rock it's made of will slice through the sole of a leather boot like it was butter or split a horse's hoof wide open. But in a fight the Leatherfeet can scamper over them rocks like lizards, and generally any one of them is a match for ten of their enemy."

"It sounds like the ideal place to make a stand," Faro agreed.

"That it is," Ashford agreed. "Leatherfoot legend has it that many many years ago, when the first Span-iards were taking over this land, they came up here with an army of nearly two thousand men, some of them conquistadors and the rest braves from neighbor-ing enemy tribes. The goal of the Spaniards was to capture the entire Leatherfoot tribe and carry them back to the coast as slaves. Five hundred Leatherfoot holed up in the lava beds, and the fighting went on for nearly four months. But when the conquistadors finally straggled off, only about a third of them were left, and they did not carry a single prisoner back with them."

"So they do know how to fight, even though they haven't particularly chosen to do so lately," Faro said.

"I would say so," Ashford told him. "They haven't fought in a long time, preferring to live in peace with the white settlers. But now, banished, desperate, and with this new chief, Burning Wind, in command, it is very likely that same fighting spirit which helped them defeat the Spaniards has been reborn."

Two days of arduous travel lay ahead of them. Occasionally they saw enough indications that the war party had passed this way to reinforce Ashford's belief that the Indians were in the lava beds, but they caught no glimpses of the Indians themselves. That suited Faro fine. He hoped that they were every one holed up in their natural fortifications, so that if the opportunity came for him to make his break, there would be no unfortunate encounters before his return to civilization.

At the end of their second day on the trail, they made their camp in a strip of pines along the banks of a small, busy stream no more than a mile or two to the east of the lava beds. As the troops were picketing their horses for the night and gathering up armloads of deadfall for their cooking fires, Ashford took Lieutenant Beale and Faro aside and explained what he had in mind to try. The lieutenant was angry and rebellious when he heard that Ashford wanted to open up negotiations between the Indians and the Army, rather than let Volney handle it in a strictly military way.

"I cannot agree to what you are proposing," Beale told the scout heatedly. "Letting you go in there alone would be a direct contradiction of my orders. I could be court-martialed or even drummed out of the service for such a thing."

"Just what exactly are the orders Volney gave you?" Ashford asked.

"You were there," Beale told him impatiently. "He told you exactly the same thing he told me. Determine the location of the enemy, then send word back to Fort Volney for support. He didn't say a damn thing about negotiating anything."

"Well, have you determined the location of the enemy?" the scout asked.

"Sure. They're right over there in those lava rocks."

"What makes you so sure? Have you seen any of them? Have you followed their trail right up to the point that it leads into the lava beds, or is there a possibility that they turned at the edge and headed north or south?"

"Well, hell, Jason. You said yourself that—"

"What if I'm wrong?" Ashford interrupted.

The scout seemed intent on creating as much doubt and confusion in the lieutenant's mind as possible, and if that was his objective, then he was apparently succeeding. Beale looked over toward the line of distant stone which rose abruptly from the surrounding level terrain, his face a mask of uncertainty.

"If I was mistaken," Ashford pressed on convincingly, "and Major Volney led his entire command out on another wild-goose chase because of word you sent back to him, that would be the surest way I know of for you to kiss those little gold bars on your shoulders good-bye. And it wouldn't help things any for me to tell him that I advised you not to send back for him so soon," he warned.

Beale was beginning to glower at Ashford, resenting the implied threat and the position it put him in, but he did not know what he could do about it.

"Let's just say I want to go in there and make sure the Indians are really there before we send word to

Volney," Ashford said. "How would that be? And then while I was there, if we just happened to start talking, and if Burning Wind just happened to agree to parley, think what a feather in your cap it would be to tell the major that not only had you located the Leatherfeet but that they had been convinced to negotiate."

"It would be, I suppose, but . . ."

Ashford rose to his feet before the lieutenant could express any further doubts. "It'll be at least an hour before full dark arrives," he said. "That should be enough time to reach the lava beds and begin looking around. Many of the braves in the tribe know me, and if they're in there, they'll see me coming. But if I don't make contact, I'll head on back here for the night and try again in the morning. Only a lamebrained fool would try to work his way into the middle of that stuff in the dark of night."

Within a few moments the scout was mounted and starting on his way eastward through the tall, thick grass which grew at the edge of the pines. But he had gone only about fifty yards when he stopped his horse and began gazing about on all sides. Then he slowly backed the animal a few steps, turned, and rode calmly back into camp.

"What's the matter?" Lieutenant Beale asked him. "You forget something?"

"No, not exactly," Ashford said. "Now, just keep your head and don't do anything rash until we figure out what's going on around here . . ."

"What in the hell are you talking about?" Beale asked impatiently.

It was not necessary for Ashford to answer. At the same instant, a host of brown-skinned forms appeared at the edge of the trees where the soldiers were. All were armed, most with rifles taken from the recent raid on the fort, but none seemed in any great hurry to employ them.

Some of the soldiers had been building their fires and others were pitching their small canvas shelters. To a man, they were caught off guard by the sudden appearance of the Indians they had come here to find.

"You be smart soldier boys," one of the Indians said, stepping forward slightly. "Don't fight, don't die."

The advice seemed sound to Faro.

"Pickets!" Lieutenant Beale mumbled heatedly, pounding his leg with his fist as if in punishment as they rode east toward the lava beds. "It's one of the first things they teach you to do on any field operation. Post your pickets! And I was going to, but I thought it wouldn't hurt for the men to get their camp made first."

"Don't worry about it," Ashford said from beside the lieutenant. "I have an idea that things are going to work out just fine like this. Maybe even better than the way I had in mind."

On the far side of the lieutenant, Faro was wondering how being captured by Indians and taken into the heart of their stronghold was such a fine thing to have happen. When they have us skinned, skewered, and ready to roast, Faro thought, Ashford will still be telling everybody to take it easy and don't panic.

All in all, though, Faro had to admit, the capture had been a rather calm and uneventful affair. After surrounding the soldiers, the forty or so Indians in the party had moved in quickly to gather up their weapons. Then they had given the troopers time to repack their gear and saddle their horses, seeming in no hurry about any of it. Later, when they all started riding through the grassland toward the lava beds, the captors had not even bothered to tie anybody's hands.

Still, though, Lieutenant Beale shared much of Faro's

cynicism about their predicament. "I don't know any-more what to make of you or the kind of advice you hand out, Ashford," he admitted. "First, when they were taking the fort, you told me to back off, not to fight, and to just sit quietly by while they ransacked the place. Then, back there, you could have sounded the alarm as soon as you rode out and spotted them coming, but instead you just turned around and rode back, calm as you please, not giving us any warning of what was about to happen."

"Don't fight, don't die," Ashford said quietly, repeat-ing the warning the Indian had given them at the camp.

"But shit!" Beale snapped. "What damn good are these guns that we have . . . er, had . . . if we never do put them to use? If you had your way, maybe the army would just pull clean on out of this corner of the state, and the ranchers and settlers with them, so this handful of dog-eating redskins could have it all back."

"That might not be such a bad notion at that," Ash-ford growled with quiet hostility.

As the party of captors and prisoners drew closer to the lava beds Faro began to examine the area with in-creasing interest as the final few threads of daylight faded behind them. They had the appearance of an ocean in the midst of a hurricane which had been some-how frozen instantly and permanently into a jagged, swirling torrent of bluish-brown rock. Rising starkly up from the flat plains around them, they appeared every bit as forbidding and defensible as Ashford had described them to be.

Once into the rocks, they were forced to leave their horses behind and continue on foot, and despite the darkness their Indian captors led the way through the twisted trails and chasms with quiet confidence. The soldiers were in a subdued mood, not knowing what sort of treatment they could expect nor what additional strokes of misfortune awaited them.

After about half an hour of travel in the darkness, the Indians led them into the round, gaping mouth of a huge cave. By the smell of wood smoke in the air, Faro guessed that they must be approaching the main encampment of the Leatherfoot. The one cave turned out to be a complex maze of passageways and tunnels. The Indians led them down one corridor after another, lighting the way with torches, until at last they reached a large open area deep within the rock.

"You wait here," the leader of the war party told the soldiers, and then, to make sure his orders were obeyed, he left half a dozen of his men there to cover them with rifles. The rest of the braves scattered in several directions, some headed back toward the entrance and others going toward the several cooking fires which dotted the huge chamber.

"This place is just incredible," Lieutenant Beale muttered.

"A scientist passing through these parts one time told me these caverns were made by fresh hot lava melting its way through the old hard crust," Ashford explained. "I bet not even these Indians, who know more about these caves than anybody else, could say exactly how far down into the earth they go."

The chamber they were facing was about a hundred feet wide and five times as long. The ceiling was in some places forty and fifty feet high, and dozens of small passageways led away from it in all directions. Some sort of natural ventilation seemed to carry the smoke from the fires harmlessly away.

In a few moments the leader of the Indian party returned. He gave some orders to his men in their own language, then turned to Ashford and said, "I told Burning Wind that the army scout Ashford was here

with soldiers, and he ordered that we bring you to him."
Faro was a little surprised at the man's ease with
English, but then he remembered Ashford's explanation
that all these Indians had lived around white men for
many years. It made sense that they would have to learn
the white man's tongue in order to get along.

"Your soldiers will be kept over there," the Indian
continued, indicating a dark passageway nearby, "but
they will not be harmed unless they try to escape or
cause trouble. You will come with me."

"And my friend Blake?" Ashford asked. "Can he
come along, too?"

"As you wish."

The Indian led the two men across the large open
area, threading his way among the campfires toward
the center of the chamber. There a number of large
stones had been gathered to form a circle about fifty
feet in diameter, and in its center a small ceremonial
fire burned. Beside the fire one Indian sat cross-legged
on the stone floor. His shoulders were covered with a
green blanket stamped U.S. Army and his head was
bowed forward as if in prayer.

"Burning Wind. They are here," the Indian announced to the motionless figure as they approached.

The man by the fire rose slowly, as if abandoning
his silent reverie only with great reluctance. Then he
stood still for another moment before finally turning to
face his two captives.

"You?" Ashford stammered in disbelief. "You're
Burning Wind?"

Chapter Nine

The tall, darkly handsome Indian stood gazing at them for a moment, obviously enjoying the expression of surprise on the face of the scout. Like most of his fellow tribesmen, he was wearing a beaded buckskin shirt and trousers, with a wide blue bandanna around his head to hold his long hair back. Finally he stepped forward and extended his hand to Ashford in a warm sign of welcome.

"I've been anticipating this moment with some delight, Jason," Burning Wind said. His English was flawless and contained no traces of Indian accent, though it did reach Faro's ears as remotely British.

"Iron Deer!" Ashford exclaimed. "My eyes are telling me it's you, but it's still hard to believe . . ."

At the mention of the name Iron Deer, Faro realized that this man must be the same wealthy Indian that Ashford had encountered during his travels abroad. But more than that, Faro thought, even he found some-

thing vaguely familiar about the features of the tall
Indian chief. Then it hit him, by God! Luigi Scirocco
and Ab Eisentier, once you took away the black whiskers or the white ones . . .

At about the same time, Ashford seemed to realize
the same thing. "And damned if that wasn't you at the
fort, too, wasn't it?" he said. "You must have had yourself a few good laughs at our expense, jawin' about your
poor busted pots and the bloody massacres you never
committed." His face was plastered with a broad grin,
and it was obvious that he considered it all a grand
joke on the army and himself.

"There were a few times that I had trouble keeping
a straight face," Burning Wind admitted. "But it all
had its serious, important side, too. We were in desperate need of guns and food in order to make our stand
here, and my little deceptions did accomplish that goal."

"But that still doesn't explain how you got from
Europe to here in California with the Leatherfoot tribe.
I didn't know you were a Leatherfoot."

"I was always deliberately vague," Burning Wind
admitted, "because nobody had ever heard of my small
nation. What mattered, what made me feel unique and
important, was that I was an American Indian, living
among the so-called cultured races of the world. What
better kind of success story could there be than to
climb up from the primitive conditions of existence
here to a life of ease and wealth in a place like Paris
or Rome?"

"It would appear so," Ashford said.

"Yes, my friend, it would appear so," Burning Wind
said. "But we both saw those places and those people,
and we both saw what kind of freak I had become.
Neither of us liked or respected me very much back
then, did we?"

"I told my friend Blake here as much no less than a week ago," Ashford admitted.

"And yet I might have remained that man, living that sort of life for the rest of my days," Burning Wind said, "had it not been for a one-page letter dictated by an old man on his deathbed nine months ago. He told of a once proud race of Indians, one of the chosen peoples of Nakokala, the Great Above-All Father, and of the humiliation and injustice they were forced to endure at the hands of the invaders of their land. Long they had waited in vain, he said, for a strong, wise leader to save them from destruction, but Nakokala had turned his face from them. They were doomed.

"That letter tugged at my heart as nothing in my life ever had before, because it was a final communication to me from my father, Bear Walks Slowly, chief of the Leatherfoot tribe. That same day I began to sell off the pieces of my shipping business, taking any price that was offered to me. Haste was much more important than money. I did not have any idea what was going on back here, because my father did not explain in detail. Nor did I deceive myself into believing that I was a man strong enough and wise enough to be leader sent by Nakokala to save my people. But I did know the white man's way, having once done my best to become as he was, and I had a supply of what the white man valued most in all the world—money. I knew I could be of some help, and when I returned to the Leatherfoot I assumed my rightful place as chief of the tribe."

"But why the Burning Wind?" Ashford asked. "What happened to Iron Deer?"

"After living so long in your world," Burning Wind said with a slight grin, "I could never equate my old name with anything but a lawn ornament. And you have to admit, my new name does have a certain ring to it. It just seemed to me that the typical names that my tribesmen are burdened with, names like Limping Squirrel and Woodpecker and Laughing Crow, wouldn't quite strike terror in the hearts of our persecutors. But Burning Wind—now, there's a monicker for you!"

"I suppose so," Ashford conceded. "But I'll have to warn you that names aren't going to strike much terror into the heart of one Major Nehemiah Volney, and he's the one you're going to have to deal with in this situation. He's back at the fort now, just itching to find you and give you what-for, especially after the Crystal Creek thing. Just exactly what is it you want, Burning Wind?"

"A simple thing," the chief said. "I want only a place where my people can live in peace and according to their customs. Look around you here and you'll see only the shadow of what we once were. Twenty years ago our tribe was twice this large, and a hundred years ago we were a thousand strong. Now we are but a scant two hundred, and our numbers decrease yearly. Our only hope for survival is to have a place of our own, at least a small inviolate homeland where our enemies do not threaten us like a ring of starving wolves."

"And where might that place be?" Ashford asked.

Burning Wind raised his hands and gestured to the chamber around him. "Here," he said, "these lava beds and a portion of the land around them. It is not prime land, the kind that any white settler would long to steal from us, but it would suffice for our needs. There are forests for fuel and meat, a stream for water, some arable soil in which to plant our meager crops. It would be enough, and we could survive in this place.

"When I raided your fort," the chief went on, "I really had two things in mind. One was food and guns and horses, and the other was to lead your soldiers here."

"Why would you want to do that?" Ashford asked.

"I figure that only a fool would try to attack and drive us from these rocks," Burning Wind reasoned. "We have held out here before against overwhelming odds and could do so again if necessary. That gives us a good bargaining position. We hope that, seeing us here, ready to fight, your commander will be willing to negotiate to give us this land and let us stay. It is all we ask."

"Only a fool would attack you," Ashford agreed wryly. "So you'd best tell your men to keep a constant lookout for Major Volney and his troops, because I can well imagine that happening soon."

"We don't want to kill anybody!" Burning Wind insisted. "It's been so long since we've been on the war-path that most of my braves don't even remember the symbols and designs they're supposed to paint on their faces to bring them good fortune in battle. They have to make them up. In the morning I'm going to release these soldiers here as an act of good faith, and I'm going to send the message back with them that I want to talk. There is no real war yet. No one has died, and there is still time to back away and negotiate. But we are willing to fight and to die before we're forced to go back to the Klamath reservation. Of that we are certain, Jason."

"It all sounds pretty desperate," Ashford said, "but I can't say as how I blame you. Hell, it might work."

"Most among us believe that it will," the chief said, "and I have a powerful ally in our tribal shamaness, Evening Star. Her magic is strong, and she holds great sway over our people. Only a few of the most rebellious young braves dare defy her . . . and me . . . with their foolish talk of annihilating the white men who have seized our land. But if I fail in this, then some of the young hotheads like Jay Feather and Woodpecker could

seize the ears of our people and lead them into a sense-
less, suicidal war."

"I'll tell the lieutenant what you said and he'll deliver
your message back to Volney," Ashford promised.

"Tell him he and his men will be freed in the morning and that their horses will be returned, but not their
guns. The Leatherfoot will wait here to talk of peace
and honor when the major comes. Go now and tell
your lieutenant. And I must go and confer with Evening
Star. We have sacred fires to burn to Nakokala and
entreaties to make. . . ."

Faro spent an uncomfortable night sleeping on the
hard stone floor of the womblike cranny where he and
the soldiers were imprisoned for the night. True to his
word, Burning Wind had the soldiers awakened early
the next morning and instructed to gather their bed-
rolls and packs for the trip back to the fort. As the
uniformed soldiers assembled behind the Indian who
would guide them out of the cave and to the edge of
the lava beds where their horses waited, Faro wondered
for perhaps the twentieth time if he had made the right
choice in deciding to stay behind. Ashford had urged
him to, but had never really offered any concrete reasons why. He just seemed to need the kind of support
that a friend could provide, and Faro, feeling no strong
inclinations to return to Fort Volney anyway, had
impulsively agreed to remain. He was as safe here, he
figured, as he would be back at the fort, what with
Marantha Volney flouncing around and seeming constantly on the verge of revealing their tryst, and to his
own surprise as much as anyone else's, Faro found himself developing a genuine interest in what lay in store
for the embattled Leatherfoot tribe.

As soon as the soldiers were gone, the guards aban-
doned Faro and Ashford and they were given the run

of the cave encampment. Almost immediately Ashford set out in search for Burning Wind for another conference, and Faro sat down near a fire to look over a week-old copy of a San Francisco newspaper which one of the soldiers had left behind.

The instant he unfolded the paper and glanced over it, the headline reached out and struck him like a hard slap in the face.

> Estrella del Norte Strike
> Heralds New Gold Boom!

Stunned, Faro read the article quickly, feeling each word of the news stab into him like a knife. It seems that one Amos "Knuckles" Harbison, local railroad magnate, had recently discovered one of the biggest gold reefs since the boom of forty-nine in his newly acquired Estrella del Norte mine. Harbison was quoted as saying that he had acquired his share in the mine as a fluke while playing poker one night, but he was now actively seeking his disappeared partner, a man named Simon Carmody, in order to share his good fortune with him.

But there was a problem with the search, Harbison had told the newspaper. He had been so drunk at the time that he remembered practically nothing about Carmody, only that Carmody possessed an engineering report on the mine. That report, Harbison explained, would be enough to establish Carmody's identity and earn him a share in the wealth. "God knows there's enough gold to go around," Harbison had said.

Faro felt a sudden urge to scream and throw himself against the stone wall nearby, but he decided that such behavior might not go over too well with the Indians around him. Instead he settled on committing violent mayhem on the newspaper and pitching it into the fire, but that brought him scant satisfaction.

Then it occurred to him that if he had snookered Harbison into buying the mine in the first place, surely there was a way to manipulate him just one more time. All he would have to do was get out of here and return to San Francisco, then . . .

He glanced up and, across the way, saw an Indian brave carefully breaking down and cleaning one of the rifles taken in the raid on the fort days earlier. Nearby, another man was painstakingly scraping a long, slender shaft of wood with a sharp, flat rock, making an arrow.

Sure, Faro thought. All he had to do was get out of here.

She was an interesting-looking woman. Her features were precise and finely formed and could as easily have belonged to a woman of Asian stock as they did to an American Indian. She appeared to be about forty years old, but her age was revealed more by the look of maturity and wisdom on her lovely features than by any sag or wrinkle on her honey-colored skin. Instead of wearing a simple buckskin dress like most of the other women of the tribe, she was clad in a complicated concoction of red cloth wrapped around her body and ornamented with numerous feathers, glass beads, animal claws, and strips of fur.

Faro stood off to one side for some time, watching her as she ground some indefinable ingredients into a fine powder in a stone bowl. He had first spotted her here in a remote corner of the cave during one of his aimless strolls and had paused to study the odd symbols and carvings on the walls, which seemed to indicate had no idea whether he should even be there, but nobody showed up to run him off.

that the area was a kind of holy place to the tribe. He

For a long time she paid him no attention, though she must have been aware of his presence. Her whole concentration was on the task before her, and as she worked she muttered a constant litany in her native tongue. Faro had never seen anything quite like it.

At last she stopped and laid the stone pestle aside; then, holding the bowl in both hands before her, she rose to her feet and turned toward him. Without speaking she closed the gap between them until they stood face to face, with the bowl raised up at chin height separating them.

"Howdy. You must be Evening Star, the shamaness that the chief was talking about yesterday," Faro said with what he hoped was a winning smile. "My name's Faro Blake and I'm . . ."

Without answering, she took a deep breath and blew the powdery contents of the bowl into his face. He immediately sneezed and coughed, trying to expel the potion from his body, but it was too late. He had already inhaled some of it. He backed away from her clumsily but stopped after a couple of steps when his shoulders collided with one of the stone walls behind him. His lungs were burning and his head was beginning to swim.

"I am the priestess Evening Star," she told him. Her voice was smooth and sensual like the coo of a morning dove.

"Well, what the . . . ?" Faro's thoughts were fragmented, and he had difficulty holding on to any single one for more than an instant. "What was that stuff?"

"I have cast the spell of the holy mushroom on you. It is the most sacred ritual of our tribal religion," she explained to him calmly. "If you are to be among us and help us in our fight to survive, then you must make this journey to understanding. And it is my task to be your guide."

At the moment, Faro felt as if the only kind of journey he was close to making was from standing up to lying down. His head was swirling like a soaring eagle in flight, and his entire body felt limber and unresponsive. Evening Star moved to his side and lifted one of his arms over her shoulder, supporting him at the very moment he would have collapsed without her help. Despite her medium height and slim frame, she was surprisingly strong. She guided him toward the rear of the cave with very little effort, which was a good thing since his rubbery feet and legs were in no mood to cooperate. She laid him on a soft pallet on the stone floor, then knelt beside him and began to gently massage his temples with her cool fingertips.

Faro's consciousness was like swirling smoke through which all the impressions of his senses floated and merged, indistinguishable from one another.

"To know us, and to understand the link between the tribe and our ancestral homeland," Evening Star crooned softly from the void around him, "is to understand the union an Indian feels with all of nature. We are one with the sky, the trees, the birds, and creatures of the forest, and to take that from us is to rob us of our very souls."

Her words were everything. They probed to his inner depths and implanted themselves in him: they became him. He understood.

"Cast away all thought. Discard your identity as a useless thing and simply feel." Her soft words were an imperative. His mind was clay, eager to be formed by her will. "To feel is to know."

There was awareness below his consciousness that the restraints and coverings were being removed from the motionless form which was his body. Warmth and weight enveloped him.

"To feel is to feel," she tutored. "Who are you?"

At the moment he could not quite recall precisely who or even what he was, but even if he had been privy to that knowledge, he could not have answered.

"Who am I?" His own voice sounded strange and hollow, an echo that rolled toward his mind from some distance away.

"You are the clouds and I am the air," she said. "I hold you within me. As you move I make a way for you, but I still contain you."

Without thought, his nervous system responded to her. His body arched and delightful sensations washed over him. He floated, held aloft by her will and reveling in the utter freedom which he felt at that moment.

"You are the mighty redwood, and I am the mother earth. Your roots are deep within me, and I nurture you because it is my function, my mission in Nakokala's plan. We do not question. We simply feel and understand.

"You are the squirrel, and I, the she-wolf, swallow you whole. Your body becomes my body, and we are one. You are the man, and I the grave. I await you, but you do not fear me, because you realize that knowing me will free your spirit."

Above him she was a shimmering blur of movement. Her voice issued from a shapeless mist of soft brown which undulated rhythmically up and down, tenderly subduing him.

"Yes, I can feel it," she moaned. *"I can feel it."* There was joy and excitement in her voice. The air was thick about them, charged with a sudden frenzy. "Erupt and create," she urged him frantically, "just as the great flowing fire once rushed up from the center of the earth and formed this holy place."

The pleasure was overwhelming. Filled to overflowing, his consciousness succumbed at last to the blackness which could be his only relief.

Though he remembered very little of it, nobody had to tell Faro what had happened to him. The evidence told the whole story as he slowly regained consciousness.

He was still on the pallet, still naked, though his body was now covered over with a light blanket from the chest down. His skin felt dank and clammy with the residue of dried sweat, and down between his legs his penis throbbed dully, telling a tale of overindulgence and misuse.

The air about him was illuminated with a pale, flickering light which he finally determined was coming from two candles sitting on a stone ledge several feet from where he lay. Slowly he rose up onto one elbow and looked around him. That was when he spotted her, no longer a dominating, ethereal spirit but now merely a flesh-and-blood woman sitting cross-legged on a square of cloth in the shadows a few feet to his left.

The faint light barely illuminated the features of her face, bare breasts, and thighs, but it seemed to impart a glowing intensity to her eyes as she stared without expression at him.

"Just what in the holy hell's been happening to me?" he demanded, rising to a sitting position on the pallet. He was half mad and half puzzled over the jumble of confusing memories which were floating around on the fringes of his mind.

"How do you feel?" the woman asked him quietly.

"Kinda used up, and kinda sore down there," he said.

"I gave you too much, I think," she told him. "I wasn't sure how you would be when you came back, or if you would even come back at all."

"Come back?" Faro asked. "Come back from where?"

"Your journey into understanding. Do you remember any of it at all?"

"Just little snatches of crazy stuff," he admitted. "Flying through the air, and thinking as how I was a tree or a squirrel or something . . . crap like that. I don't know what that stuff was that you gave me, but it was the most ass-kicking Mickey I've ever seen. The Shanghai gangs down in Frisco would give a pretty to get their hands on some of that stuff, I'll wager."

"Because you came to us as a friend, wishing only well to us," Evening Star explained, "Chief Burning Wind ordered that you be initiated into the tribe as an honorary brother. The powder I gave you was the dust of the sacred mushrooms, blended with a mixture of secret herbs to open your mind to understanding. Now you are one of us in spirit, no longer an enemy to be mistrusted and held captive. It was the will of the chief, and was agreed to by the other white brother, Jason Ashford."

Faro didn't understand much of anything she was saying, but he figured that if Ashford approved it, he must have known that it would not be harmful or deadly. He glanced around the area one more time and spotted his clothes in a jumbled pile nearby, then started to rise.

"Well, I thank you, ma'am," he said, "though for what I ain't quite certain. But if you're through stupefying and mystifying me for one day, I s'pose I'll be moving on out of here."

By the time he was standing, she was on her feet, too, and moving in his direction. As she came into a patch of better light he noted what a sleek and finely formed body she had. She moved with a smooth grace, seeming unaware of both their naked conditions as she stepped up quite close to him.

"The sacred ceremony is over," she said, raising one hand up and letting her fingers dance lightly across his chest, "but you still might be interested in learning more about some of our ways and customs." She let her fingers roam up to trace the shape of his lips as she eased forward and grazed her nipples gently against his chest.

"I might be, at that," he allowed with a grin.

When Faro emerged from Evening Star's sanctuary some two hours later, he was sated, slack-jawed, and plodding with fatigue after the bizarre and exotic experiences he had gone through in her clutches. He had no idea what hour of the day or night it was, nor did he really care. First on his agenda was a little food to lessen the pangs of hunger which were gnawing at his middle, and second was a few hours of rest. And after that . . . well, the way things had been going lately, who could tell?

Chapter Ten

Faro was roughly awakened by a hand shaking his shoulder and a voice hissing urgently in his ear, "Wake up, old son! There's big doin's amongst the Leatherfeet, I'm afraid!"

As Faro opened his eyes and rolled over he saw Ashford kneeling over him, prodding him awake. Faro sat on up on his blanket and reached for his boots. "What time is it?" he asked. "It's damned aggravating never quite knowing the difference betwixt day and night in this fucking cave."

"Nighttime, daytime, or a freckle past midnight," Ashford said tensely, "it don't make a damned bit of difference to what's going on out there right now."

"What is going on?" Faro asked. He glanced out into the main chamber and saw that most of the Indians there were gathering around the large circle of rocks in the center.

"I ain't sure," Ashford told him.

"Shit, Jason!" Faro complained. "You're not going to start back up with all the riddles and suchlike again, are you? I'm bound to tell you that I'm just not in the mood for those kinds of carryings-on at the moment."

"I can just tell that there's trouble of some kind afoot by the way everybody's acting. A while ago several of the braves that had been scouting came back, and the two called Woodpecker and Jay Feather went straight in to see Burning Wind in his lean-to. Then, not five minutes after, Burning Wind sent the word out that he was calling a council of the whole tribe."

"Well, let's just amble down there and see what it's all about," Faro suggested. "You speak enough of their lingo to get the gist of things, don't you?"

"I do, but I've got sense enough not to go down there right now," Ashford said. "If you'll remember, it was Woodpecker and Jay Feather that Burning Wind mentioned as preferring dead white folks over live ones."

"But aren't we blood brothers now?" Faro asked only half teasingly. Evening Star had seemed serious when she told him he was a brother, though he had to admit that he and she had not acted in a very brotherly and sisterly fashion with each other.

"Remember how Cain slew his brother Abel in the Good Book?" Ashford said. "Well, I got a notion that these two ain't got nothing up on Adam's boys. From the distance I saw them at when they came in, it looked to me like they were carrying coups, but right now I don't feel much like going down and verifying that close up. No, sir, I think I'll stay up here and catch what I can of the talk at a distance."

Within a few minutes, when all the Indians were assembled, Burning Wind stood up before them. In loud, angry tones which could be heard clearly even as far away as where Faro and Ashford were, he started to address the tribe in their native tongue. After the first few words, the scout began to quietly translate for Faro.

"He's reminding them," Ashford said, "of the day when he came back home and began giving them hope and pride again. He's telling them to remember back to how things were on the reservation, of the fear and misery and humiliation there. When he returned, he says, he brought with him a plan to get them away from the reservation, to gain them a place in their own homeland.

"But now, he says, some young rebels in the tribe have taken their real pride and turned it into false pride. They have taken the tribe's hope and turned it into ashes by killing and scalping three white soldiers who were promised safety until they returned to Fort Volney."

"Oh, shit!" Faro muttered under his breath.

The grim look on Ashford's face showed that he agreed with the sentiment. "Burning Wind says," the scout went on, "that by tribal law he cannot turn these braves over to the white soldiers. He and the whole tribe must accept the responsibility for the deeds of the few. But if it is the will of the entire tribe, the ringleaders can be exiled. It is for all to decide."

When the chief was finished, the two leaders of the scalping party stepped forward to give their side of things, and their speech soon turned into an extended narrative of how they had bravely ambushed the unarmed soldiers and scalped three of them while the others scattered into the brush in terror. "We are proud warriors again!" Woodpecker exclaimed passionately at the end of the account. "Now no one can call the Leatherfoot cowards or old women again!"

"No, but they can just about call the Leatherfoot dead!" Faro said in response to Ashford's translation.

A lengthy debate followed, and even though Ashford finally tired of translating, Faro had already pretty well deciphered the tone of the affair. Though much of the tribe remained behind Burning Wind and his aims for them, a solid core of the younger warriors condoned the actions of Woodpecker and Jay Feather and praised them for the scalpings. Galled by the idea of having to scrape a living out of the miserable parcel of land that Burning Wind hoped to gain for the tribe, they began to call out in the fieriest language for a fight to the death—their own, their women's and children's, and for that matter, Faro realized grimly, his and Ashford's, too.

Three tense days passed as the Leatherfeet made preparations for the attack which they knew must surely follow the scalping of the three men in Volney's command. Hunting parties were out day and night scouting the surrounding countryside for game, and what women in the tribe who were not employed in slicing the meat into long thin strips and drying it into jerky atop the lava rocks were sent out to gather roots, grain, berries, and whatever other natural staples they could glean from the land. Scores of ancient earthenware pots, traditionally kept in the caves by the tribe, were scrubbed out, refilled with fresh water from the stream a mile away, and hauled back for storage in the caves.

Faro quickly began to notice a drastic change in the way he and Ashford were treated. They still were not guarded and were permitted to roam the caves at will, but anytime they ventured outside, they were closely watched. A bullet in the back would be his reward, he figured, for the first indication that he was trying to make his way out of the lava beds.

Major Volney and his entire command showed up

late on the evening of the third day and took up positions in the flatlands to the west, just beyond the range
of a rifle bullet from the edge of the lava beds. Shortly
before dusk, Faro and Ashford accompanied Burning
Wind and most of the men in the tribe as they went out
to survey the "enemy."

As Faro and Ashford crouched on a promontory
slightly apart from the Indians, Faro mumbled dis-
gruntledly to his companion, "Brother, I been in some
rotten situations in my time, but I think this one just
about takes the prize. We oughta be out there, dammit!
Not in here!"

"Yeah, I reckon," Ashford said thoughtfully. His
mood had darkened again as the prospect of an im-
pending battle increased. There were just entirely too
many ways for a man to end up dead around this
place.

Volney and his men had made their camp facing
the lava beds along a two-hundred-yard front, and
their intentions seemed obvious. No negotiators were
being sent forward under white flags of truce, and
through a spyglass borrowed from Ashford Faro saw
that all of the fort's artillery had been brought along:
four iron cannons mounted on wheeled carriages.
Volney would have his fight at last.

At dawn the next morning Major Volney signaled
the commencement of battle in the standard military
way. The cannons were moved forward to within a
half mile of the lava beds, and for an hour they
pounded away at the rocks at the edge of the Indian
stronghold in an effort to soften up resistance. Actually,
though, they did very little damage. The hard volcanic
stone seemed practically impervious to the blasts of
the small cannonballs, and Volney's artillerymen had
no specific targets. Only a couple of Indians were

killed by lucky direct hits, and half a dozen others were slightly wounded by flying shards of stone and iron.

Finally, though, the cannons fell silent and a momentary lull ensued. The air was charged with expectancy, and Faro and Ashford, crouching along the rocks, waited grimly along with the Indians to see what would come next.

Soon long lines of blue-clad figures charging on horseback out of the thick morning mist toward the lava outcroppings came into view.

"Dammit, Volney, you asshole!" Ashford complained bitterly. "This is stupid. Stupid! Don't you remember anything I told you about these Leatherfoot and their lava beds? Don't you know these poor sons of bitches are going to cut to pieces before they even lay eyes on the first Indian?"

"Apparently not," Faro muttered dourly.

When the soldiers got about a quarter mile from their objective, the Leatherfoot started to use their captured army rifles to empty saddles with rhythmic precision. Within a couple of minutes the charge was blunted, and soon after the surviving troopers turned their mounts and retreated in chaos. When the smoke and confusion cleared, Faro and Ashford saw the bodies of twoscore dead and dying soldiers littering the battlefield before them.

Through the spyglass Faro spotted Volney about half a mile away, frantic with anger as he attempted to rally his fleeing soldiers for a second charge. It took him a few minutes, but at last he got it done, and soon another wave of mounted men began to race suicidally forward, screaming horribly at the tops of their lungs as they fired their guns futilely at their hidden foe. Immediately the Indian rifles spoke again and the carnage of the first charge was repeated.

"Dammit all!" Ashford exclaimed in despair. "I could strangle that bastard with my own two hands! What does he think he's doing? What has all this accomplished?"

Just as before, this second charge dissolved in disarray and the soldiers fell back, leaving a new flock of dead and wounded to join their previously fallen compatriots.

"Not again!" Ashford shouted at the top of his lungs. "For God's sake, Volney, not again!" The soldiers were too far away to hear, but soon it was apparent that the major had come to the same conclusion on his own. For a while the Indians occupied themselves with pumping bullets into anything that moved as the soldiers milled around in temporary confusion, then began to fall back to safer distance. Faro searched for a glimpse of Volney through the spyglass but could not find him again.

"Come on, Blake," Ashford ordered decisively. "Let's go find Burning Wind." They scrambled down off the rock they had been lying atop, then began working their way north through ragged, rocky passageways.

They found the chief crouching in a slight depression, conferring with half a dozen of his braves. As the two white men approached, the other Indians glanced up at them distrustfully, but Burning Wind gave an order which dispersed them in several directions. Then the chief raised his head and looked up at Faro and Ashford, a melancholy and searching expression on his features.

"What sort of man is he, this Major Volney?" he asked. "He must be utterly insane to waste so many lives on such a ridiculous charge. What did he hope to accomplish, and why didn't he at least give us a chance to talk first? We had no choice but to slaughter them."

"As long as I been around him," Faro said, "I can't recall seeing any signs of good sense in Volney. But this today, hell, it's nothing short of criminal."

"He's out for glory, pure and simple," Ashford said bitterly. "And it looks to me like he wouldn't mind sacrificing all the lives of his men, as well as this whole tribe, to get it."

"I see no glory for either side in what happened this morning," Burning Wind said. "None of those men need have died. It accomplished nothing for my people, and certainly nothing for the army. It only set in stone the hatred of each side for the other."

"Yeah, but one thing's certain," Ashford added. "After this, Volney would be hard put to muster up half a dozen men willing to make that kind of charge again. After this, he'll have to try some other tactic. But God only knows what it'll be."

"So we may still have our stalemate," Burning Wind said thoughtfully, "though it was bought at a bloodier price than I had hoped."

"You might, at that," Ashford said. "But it's hard to predict what state of mind Volney might be in right now."

"Listen, Jason," Faro spoke up. "Remember, after he got back from Crystal Creek a few days ago, how willing he was to listen to you then? Well, it might be the same way now. After all this he's bound to have some serious doubts about his own good judgment, and right now I'd bet he doesn't have any more idea what he's going to do next than we do. It might be the ideal time to get to him and try to talk some sense into his thick skull."

Ashford stared at him for a long moment, weighing his suggestion. He looked doubtful, but both of them knew it was about the only option they had right now.

If there was no communication, then the only thing which could logically follow was more fighting.

"Okay, Faro," the scout said at last. "We'll try it . . . that is, with Burning Wind's permission. Don't forget, we still need his say-so before we can leave these rocks."

"Yes, go. Go!" the chief told them decisively. "It can do no harm, and it might do some good. I will send the order out to all my braves not to molest you."

It was no pleasant prospect to be walking out between two armed bands which had just fought a bloody battle, but Faro knew that the smartest thing for him was to accompany Ashford on the peace mission. Whatever else might happen, he knew that the place for him was on that side of the battle rather than this side. It was a damned unsettling feeling lying on the rocks in the midst of a bunch of hostile Indians, mushroom brothers or no, watching soldiers from his own country charge at him.

Reluctantly he surrendered his white shirt for Ashford to use in fashioning a flag of truce, and soon the two of them were scrambling down out of the rocks and passing through the scattered carnage of dead men and horses toward the army lines. It was a long, tense walk, and the whole time Faro felt as if the sights from two or three hundred guns were trained at various locations on his back and chest. All the while, Ashford constantly waved the empty rifle onto which he had tied Faro's shirt.

When they got within two hundred yards of the army lines, a soldier called out for them to halt while he sent for the major. Soon Volney appeared from somewhere to the rear, his gaze burning furiously as he stared out across the space which separated them.

Without waiting to hear why they had come, he announced brusquely, "Under the circumstances, I cannot help but consider you two men as traitors. As of this moment, both of you are under arrest, and you may expect to be dealt with in only the harshest of terms."

"Now, wait just a damn minute, Major," Ashford barked back at him. "I don't know what kind of crazy notions you've got about us, but we came out here carrying a message from Burning Wind. He wants to talk so that both sides can put an end to this fighting."

"I'm not interested in hearing any talk from traitorous scum like you two," Volney said. "Lieutenant Beale has told me the whole story of how you two deserted him and his men, and about how they were sent out unarmed, only to be attacked a short time later. Three soldiers of the United States Army were killed in that ambush, and I mean for their deaths to be avenged with blood."

"Is this your kind of vengeance, you pea-brained spawn of a cross-eyed jackass?" Ashford ranted, indicating the littered battlefield behind him. "How many men are you willing to lose before you finally admit that you don't know anything more about dealing with Indians than a fish does about flying?"

"I said you're under arrest, Ashford!" Volney screamed hysterically. "Get over here and surrender yourselves immediately!"

"Fuck that!" Ashford announced firmly. When he turned and began to march decisively away, Faro had no choice but to join him.

But immediately they heard Volney scream from behind them, "Shoot those two men! Kill them! I'll have their heads on a pole in front of my tent before this thing's over."

Faro and Ashford were on the run even before the sound of the first shot rang out around them. "The grass, the grass!" Ashford shouted to Faro, pointing to a patch of tall, thick grass off to their right. But the directions were unnecessary. Faro was already springing in that direction, running in a frantic zig-zag pattern as a hail of bullets sliced the air all around them.

When he reached the sanctuary of the grass he dived down out of sight, then crawled forward on his belly. He heard Ashford doing the same off to his left. The shooting did not stop, but since the soldiers could no longer see them, their shots were not nearly as great a threat.

The paths of the two men converged a couple of hundred yards from the edge of the lava beds, and they paused for a moment to catch their breath. By now the firing from behind had ceased altogether.

"I sure botched that one good, didn't I?" Ashford said. "My temper just got away from me before I knew what was happening."

"I wouldn't hardly fault you for it," Faro said, "and besides, once that moron started talking about arrest and all, I kinda got out of the mood to go back, anyway. Seems like we're safer sticking with the Indians."

As if to contradict his statement, a shot rang out from the lava beds far to the right, beyond where any of Burning Wind's men had been stationed earlier. It hissed through the grass entirely too close to them and embedded itself in the ground with a dull thwump.

"I ain't so sure," Ashford barked as he rolled quickly to the side and leaped to his feet on the run. As they sprinted across the last hundred yards of open area three more shots landed nearby them, but they made it to the safety of the base of the rocks unharmed. Then, as the two of them crouched in a crevice, out of sight from the Indians above, Ashford shouted out, "Burning Wind! What the hell's going on?"

After a moment's pause, the chief called down to

them, "I don't know who fired those shots. Climb on
up and you won't be harmed."

Trusting the chief's word, they started cautiously
into the rocks and eventually located the place where
Burning Wind was sitting. "I don't know who dis-
obeyed me and shot at you," he said. "But I intend to
find out and deal with them."

"I got my own ideas about it," Ashford said angrily.

"Give us a couple of guns and we'll take care of the
matter for you, chief," Faro added. "I'm in just the
right state of mind at this moment to pluck myself a
peckerwood and a jaybird."

"No," Burning Wind said decisively. "I've sent men
over in that direction, and if it was Woodpecker and
Jay Feather who shot at you, they'll be brought before
me to answer for their actions. In a time of war, dis-
obeying the orders of the chief is considered one of
the most serious offenses in tribal law. Even the other
rebellious followers of those two would not back them
in such a thing."

"If you say so," Faro said. He was not at all happy
about the decision, but he realized how dangerous it
would be to cross the chief in this, no matter how
sweet the taste of revenge might be.

But his irritation increased considerably when the
men Burning Wind had sent out returned some time
later with the news that they could not locate the two
renegades.

"We found where they had been," one of the Indians
said, displaying a handful of empty cartridge casings,
"but by the time we got there, they had disappeared."

Burning Wind ordered that the search be halted,
knowing that in the expanse of tangled volcanic rocks
there were thousands of places where one or two men
might hide and never be found even by members of
their own tribe. It would be a wasted effort to go on

looking for them, and he needed every available man to keep up the vigil on the rocks facing the soldiers.

But word went out of what Woodpecker and Jay Feather had done. They would be outcasts now, ostracized from the tribe by their own deeds and subject to harsh punishment if they ever decided to return. It wasn't really punishment enough to satisfy Faro, but it was the best that was available under the circumstances. At last he and Ashford started back toward the caves in search of food and rest after their ordeal.

Chapter Eleven

A tense afternoon and night of inactivity ensued. For a while, at least, it seemed as if Volney might have given up on trying to dislodge the Indians from their fortified stronghold, which was undoubtedly a wise decision in the light of his clumsy and costly efforts earlier. For the Indians' part, there was little they could do but watch and wait—they were not about to launch an attack of their own, but they felt prepared for anything Volney might throw at them.

Faro spent the entire time inside the caves. For him to be out on the rocks watching the soldiers was not only useless and somewhat frustrating but perhaps also a little dangerous. Woodpecker and Jay Feather might still be lurking about, looking for an opportunity to finish what they had left undone that morning.

He went once in search of Evening Star, thinking that perhaps he might find the opportunity to pass some of the time pleasantly with her in the back of her ritual

chamber, but an old crone told him that the priestess
was out of the cave gathering herbs and mushrooms
for some sort of ceremony which Burning Wind had
ordered.

On the second day after the attack, the artillery
fire began again in the distance, its sound rumbling
through to the inhabitants of the cave like the shock
waves of some distant earthquake. Faro was determined to stick it out in the caverns this time, since
there was no good reason for him to do otherwise. But
finally, after a few hours, his curiosity over what Volney was up to began to get the best of him. He threaded
his way out of the caves and across the rugged stretch
of stony wasteland to the edge of the lava beds.

He found Ashford in a position near the one from
which they had watched the attack two days before.
The expression on the scout's face was even grimmer
and more embittered, and his left arm and shoulder
were bloodied where shards of rock had sliced through
his leather clothing and penetrated his skin.

"It's pretty rough out here," Ashford told Faro.
"You would have been smarter to stay back in the
caves where you were."

"I know," Faro told him, "but the waiting got to
me. What's going on?"

"One hell of a lot of artillery fire is what's going on,"
the scout said. "Just take a gander down there."

In the open area below, Faro saw how Volney's
men had been spending their time during the two-day
lull. Back in the belt of pines, they had cut logs and
built four large barricades, each about ten feet square,
with a hole in the center large enough for the muzzle
of a cannon to protrude. These had been moved forward quite near the edge of the lava beds and set into
place, and then the cannons were brought up behind
them. Instead of firing directly against the facing edge

of the lava, the artillerymen could now arch their rounds high into the air and land them back where the Indian defenders were hidden.

"It looks like somebody down there has finally started using their head for something more than a hatrack," Faro said.

"It's working, too," Ashford said. "Burning Wind has already lost half a dozen men. For a while I couldn't figure out how Volney's men seemed to know just what targets to aim at, and then I spotted the reason why. Here, take the glass and keep it on that third barricade in line awhile."

Faro did as Ashford instructed. At first he did not know what the scout was talking about, but then, after the cannon fired, he understood. Immediately after the round landed, he saw a bare-chested, dark-haired figure step out from behind the barricade momentarily and study where the round hit. It was Jay Feather.

As Faro watched, the Indian pointed toward the lava beds and said something to the soldiers behind the barricade. Then he stepped back out of sight as the crew reloaded and adjusted the angle of the cannon.

"That rotten son of a bitch," Faro exclaimed. "He's spotting the defensive positions for Volney's artillery crews!"

"You betcha," Ashford said bitterly. "And Woodpecker is down there, too, behind the barricade on the far right. Burning Wind is fit to be tied, but right now there's not one hell of a lot he can do about it. He and his lieutenants are meeting over there right now to talk over the situation."

So, for all their tough talk about tribal honor and fighting to the death, Faro thought, the two renegade Leatherfeet had finally shown their true colors in the pinch—and it wasn't red but more the shade of the stripes on a yellow jacket's tail. They had caused this whole disaster in the first place by killing and scalping the three unarmed troopers, and now that things looked grim for the tribe, they were betraying their own people to throw in with the winning side. The way they saw it, Faro figured, the only good Indian was a live Indian, and they meant to be just that.

Over the next few hours, the artillery fire continued with devastating effectiveness. After losing three or four more men to the deadly explosive cannonade, Burning Wind finally pulled his forces back to the caves, leaving only half a dozen sentries out to keep an eye on the enemy activities.

Darkness was approaching as Faro and Ashford neared the caves, and in the distance the cannon fire was beginning to abate.

"Do you think Volney will try another attack once he's softened us up with artillery?" Faro asked the scout. He was uncomfortable with the word *us,* but he had no delusions about which side the soldiers would consider him on if they did launch another attack.

"Maybe he will," Ashford speculated. "But by now I expect he realizes how heavy his casualties would be. My guess is that he's sent out for reinforcements now that he thinks he's got the Leatherfoot cornered. There's close to five hundred troops stationed at the garrison down at Enterprise, and another seven hundred or so up at Fort Klamath just over the line into Oregon. If either of those places, or both, sent help, he could double or triple his strength in a matter of days, and to my best reckoning, Burning Wind only has about seventy good fighting men still on their feet."

But despite the scout's discouraging forecast, the mood of the Indians in the cavern seemed surprisingly good. Faro saw that sometime while he was out Evening Star had returned, and now, with the aid of a young woman who seemed to be some sort of protegée, she was preparing another of her concoctions in a large iron pot in the center area of the main chamber. Nearby, over a second fire, three older women were cooking up a delightful-smelling venison stew. Burning Wind was close by, watching the preparations with silent approval, when the two white men approached.

"What's cooking?" Faro asked as they stopped by the chief to watch the women work.

"The women are preparing for a tribal victory celebration," Burning Wind informed them.

"A victory celebration?" Ashford asked. "What victory?"

"Well, I'm bending tradition somewhat for the sake of my people," the chief admitted candidly. "I know it's stretching things a bit, but they need something like this to renew their spirits. And, in a way, just holding out this long could be considered a victory of sorts. And besides," he added soberly, "we might as well hold this celebration now, because I am afraid the Leatherfoot could well have seen their last true victory for all times."

"Kind of an 'eat, drink, and be merry' thing," Faro said.

"Yes," the chief said, "because we might soon live out the second part of that quotation. 'For tomorrow we die.'"

As soon as the pots came to a lively boil, the women made their way toward the back of the cave and disappeared into a number of small passageways. Only a few old women remained to serve the men, who were starting to take seats in a large circle around the two fires.

The whole assemblage seemed to take on an eerie, almost mystical quality. The men talked very little, accepting bowls of stew as the women served it and sipping solemnly the cups of Evening Star's brew which were passed around the circle. The two white men took seats on the ground on Burning Wind's left, and when a cup finally came to Faro, he held it a moment, eyeing its contents suspiciously. He had no desire whatsoever to end up in the same kind of shape he had the first day he was subjected to Evening Star's powerful potions.

When Burning Wind saw him waver, he said, "Don't worry, my friend. It's diluted. I think you will find the results much different than they were the other time."

"If you say so," Faro muttered, still doubtful. He touched the cup to his lips and took a small sip. It tasted faintly like some sort of spicy, exotic soup.

"A little more," Burning Wind grinned. "You won't regret it."

After taking a healthy swallow, Faro passed the cup on to the chief, who downed half its contents before sending it on.

The thick deer-meat stew was a delight after the sparse rations they had been eating over the past few days. When the soldiers had first arrived days before, Burning Wind immediately ordered that everyone eat as little as possible to conserve the food stores, but tonight no one seemed to be worrying about it. Faro was well into his second bowl and had already indulged in three more swallows from the circulating cups by the time he noticed Evening Star's potion taking effect, not only on himself but on all the other men around him as well.

There were smiles all around the fire, and the men were laughing and talking gaily, as if all thoughts of the enemy outside were forgotten. For his own part, Faro was beginning to experience a delicious feeling of euphoria. Of all the problems and worries which had burdened him down over the past few days, none seemed very important now. The hundreds of soldiers outside, armed with rifles and bayonets and cannons, didn't seem to be much of a hazard anymore, and their presence was easily dismissed.

Soon the question why all the women in the tribe had disappeared was answered when a number of flaming torches appeared at the back of the cave. They assembled outside the passageways where they had gone, then started toward the men in a long, brightly lit procession. It took Faro a while to figure out why they all looked so different now, but as they neared it became more obvious.

All the Leatherfoot women from about age fifteen to fifty had stripped off their clothes and painted their bodies in a dazzling array of colors. Blue breasts bobbed enticingly with gentle steps, red bellies glistened in the light of torches held aloft by yellow and green arms, and purple legs propelled them forward to the ceremony. The application and designs of the paint seemed limited only by the imagination of the wearers. And over each of their heads the women wore hoods and headdresses designed to depict the various animals which lived in the surrounding forests. The effect was exotic and stunning.

As they entered the circle of men the women pitched their torches in a huge pile in the center, and then started to dance wildly around the ever-growing bonfire. Their shadows, magnified many times over, sped around the distant walls like so many frantic apparitions, adding to the supernatural atmosphere of the performance.

Faro, grinning like a dazed lunatic, watched it all with stupefied delight. Never before in his life, he thought, had he seen such an assemblage of bouncing, bobbling, tantalizing female flesh. The dance continued for some minutes to the uproarious accompaniment of cheers and laughter from the men, but finally one form broke away and raced over to the edge of the ring. Her shapely body was adorned with delicious splashes of every color in the rainbow, and on her head she wore a replica of a doe's head. She took Burning Wind by the hand and tugged him to his feet, then led him out into the center where a dozen women were waiting to pounce on him.

It took them only a moment to strip his clothes away and smear his body with paint from head to foot, and then, in a surprising display of abandon, the chief began a twisting, gyrating dance of his own, much to the amusement of his female attackers. Meanwhile, all around the ring various other men were receiving similar treatment.

Faro wasn't quite sure how to respond when finally a mountain lioness with a suspiciously familiar shape rushed in his direction and took his hand, pulling insistently until he rose. Close on her heels came several other laughing, squealing women, and what seemed like dozens of hands began immediately to tear the black suit from his body. Then, when he was naked, fingers began smearing him with a thick, colorful coating of paint from head to foot.

By the time they were finished and had turned to give the same treatment to Ashford, Faro was utterly caught up in the delirium of the ceremony. He made a grab for the lioness who had first drawn him forward, but she spun laughingly out of reach and danced away, with Faro giving enthusiastic pursuit.

The chase lasted for two full turns around the bonfire, but at last he enveloped his prey in his arms and they tumbled to the floor. He hardly noticed the scraping of his knees and elbows on the rough surface of the cave floor—his rigid member, protruding straight out from his body now and throbbing wildly, was doing all his thinking for him.

The woman was lying on her back before him, her legs spread invitingly, but as he poised himself, hungry to penetrate her, she said, "Not here, white brother. This rock will cut my back to pieces. Come. I have a place prepared." It was the voice of the very woman he would have chosen from all those available here— Evening Star.

When they were back on their feet, she took his hand and scampered through the crowd of revelers, headed, he soon realized, toward the familiar sanctuary of her personal chamber. The minute she cast aside the lioness disguise and dropped down on her pallet there, Faro was on top of her and entered her with one eager thrust. They screwed madly like two wild creatures rutting in the forest, slapping their bodies together in mindless frenzy.

The end came like a blast from one of Volney's cannons and left Faro spent and gasping for air. Below him Evening Star was shuddering convulsively, as if her body had been seized by the same primal forces which had created these caverns in which they now lay. He felt as if he were positioned atop a volcano about to erupt, but he lacked the energy to roll aside to safety.

In slow stages her quivering began to abate, until at last she lay motionless beneath him. Lubricated by the paint on both their bodies, Faro slid himself off of her and to the side.

When Evening Star began to rise and don her lioness headdress again, Faro raised up onto one elbow and asked, "Do we have to leave just now?"

"You stay here," she told him as her smiling face disappeared behind the costume. "And soon you may get a visit from a dove or a deer, or perhaps an antelope. Who knows what forest creature may decide to wander back this way and risk a shot from you?"

When she was gone, Faro lay back on the pallet with a contented sigh. He could never grow tired of sinking his arrow into this kind of game, he thought.

When Faro awoke, he lay for a long time studying the lovely form of the young woman who lay sleeping beside him in the dim candlelight of Evening Star's chamber. She was about nineteen or twenty, and he had seen her many times around the cave, performing her menial chores, but he had never guessed that she had this kind of tantalizing frame concealed beneath her shapeless buckskin dress.

She had been the fourth—or was it the fifth—woman to come back to where he lay, and he could only guess that the mushroom potion Evening Star had served up must have had some aphrodisiac qualities, because none of his visitors had been disappointed.

Even now, with her body paint smeared and blended chaotically across her skin, the young woman still looked tempting, and Faro wondered with amusement how far along he could get before she woke and realized what was going on. If his touch was gentle enough, he believed he could part her legs and position himself above her, and then . . .

"Blake? You come to yet?" The voice was Ashford's, and it came toward him from down the passageway leading to the main chamber. In a moment the scout came into view and stopped a few feet away to study Faro, who had just begun his preparations on his young companion.

"Hellfire, man! Ain't you had enough yet?" Ashford asked.

"You ever met a man worth his salt that did?" Faro grinned up at him.

"Maybe not," Ashford said. "But I'm afraid you're going to have to pass it up this time. Burning Wind's called a powwow, and he wants you and me there. Here, I found your clothes, such as there is left of them."

He pitched Faro a bundle of tattered cloth which had been until a few hours ago a decent black suit and a ruffled white shirt. Only the pair of boots the wad of rags were wrapped around remained usable from the entire outfit he had been wearing when the Leatherfoot "ceremony" began.

"I found your wallet and that little popgun of yours and stuck them down in the toe of one of the boots," Ashford said. "I hope you've got yourself some more duds in that valise of yours back across the way."

"Yeah, I've got some extras," Faro said as he slipped on the tattered trousers to wear until he got to his other clothes.

Ashford went along with Faro as he left Evening Star's chamber and walked across to the place where he had left his valise and case of advantage tools. There he cleaned the paint off himself as best he could with the remnants of his shredded outfit, then dressed in the extra underclothes, suit, while shirt, and socks which he carried in his valise.

"What time of day you figure it is?" Faro asked as he pulled on his boots and slipped the little Reid's derringer down into its familiar place in the pocket of his vest.

"It's near dawn," Ashford said. "I been outside already checking things out, and everything seems just about like it was last night. When daylight gets here, I figure Volney will start up with those cannons again. That's what Burning Wind wants to parley about."

By the time they located Burning Wind, he had already assembled several of his braves and was beginning to discuss the situation with them. One of the braves reported that several wagons had arrived from Fort Volney during the night, bringing fresh stores of gunpowder and cannonballs. Today promised to bring a repeat of the same incessant bombardment.

"My brothers," Burning Wind announced bitterly to the men around him, "my plan has failed. I see now that the white soldiers will never give us a chance to talk and negotiate. All that is left for us is to go on fighting until there are no more of us left for them to kill. We all knew this possibility faced us when we left the reservation, but I think all of our people will still agree that an honorable death in battle is better than life at that place."

"Why is that your only option?" Faro asked. "Volney doesn't have you completely surrounded yet. Why don't you just hightail it out of here on the far side of the lava beds?"

"We have no place to go," Burning Wind said. "To the south, east, and west there are settlers who would betray us, and to the north there are other, stronger tribes of Indians who hate us. Here, at least, when we perish we will have the satisfaction of taking many of the white soldiers with us to the grave."

"Hell, there's always Canada," Ashford suggested. "I hear tell how there's thousands of square miles of virgin territory that no men, white or red, have ever laid claim to. The Leatherfeet would be safe there."

Burning Wind simply shrugged. "None of our people knows anything about Canada," he said. "All we know is that it is to the north, on the far side of territory controlled by the Nez Perces, the Crow, the Sioux, the Blackfeet . . . To wander blindly into the homelands of these enemies would be like running a gauntlet blindfolded. Few if any of us would survive."

"I know that country from my army days, though, Burning Wind," Ashford said. "I know the rivers, the trails, the tribes that can be relied on, the best routes to avoid the settlements along the way. It seems like my days of scouting in this part of the country are over with, so I might as well go along and lead you on the trip north."

"Would it be possible?" Burning Wind asked with a sudden spark of hope.

"It's a better bet than sticking here and getting picked off one by one while your women and children hide back in the caves, starving to death. You might take aplenty of the white soldiers with you along the way, but that kind of satisfaction wouldn't be much good to you if none of you were alive to enjoy it."

The chief discussed the proposal with his braves, and all gave it their enthusiastic approval.

"All right, the first problem," Ashford said, "is how to get away from these lava beds and throw Volney's men off the trail long enough for the tribe to get out of his reach. As soon as you're gone, he'll find out quick enough, and then he'll be hot on your trail."

Faro had been silent during much of the discussion, but finally he spoke up to ask, "Burning Wind, do you still have the horses you took during the raid on the fort?"

"They're hidden in a small canyon north of here," the chief said. "Volney's men have not searched enough to find them yet."

"Well, I remember Ashford telling me how easy it is to follow the trail of horses," Faro said, "and how hard it is to follow Indians afoot. What if some of your men took the horses and started in some direc-

tion that the tribe might be expected to travel, like
south to the settlement at Crystal Creek, for instance?
Then at the same time the tribe could start out north
on foot. If Volney decided to chase after the horses, as
any dull-witted moron like him would be expected to
do in a case like this, it should give you some extra
time to get away."

"Sure, that might work," Ashford agreed enthusiastically. "We could even strap travois onto some of the
animals and load them down with rocks. It would leave
exactly the same kind of trail as if the tribe was moving their goods along, too. And even if the scheme
gained us no more than two or three days, that would
give us enough time to get across the line into Oregon."

The plan was worked out quickly. A small party of
warriors would lead the tribe's horse herd southeast
toward Crystal Creek for at least a full day, leaving a
clear trail for the soldiers to follow. Then they would
turn the horses loose and start back north, heading
toward a rendezvous with the main party, which Ashford would be guiding on its way north. Money which
Burning Wind still had left from the sale of his shipping business could be used later to buy more horses
from some source Ashford determined was safe.

During the day, as Volney's cannons continued their
pounding to the west, several braves brought the horse
herd around to the eastern side of the lava beds and
rigged travois on them for the trip south. Then in late
afternoon the other members of the tribe left the caves
and moved to the eastern side of their stone fortifications in preparation for their flight north.

Faro decided to lighten his load by leaving his
empty valise behind, but he brought along his case of
advantage tools, which still contained his only means
of livelihood. Shortly before leaving he had taken out

the stubby sawed-off shotgun, removed the rolls of money from the barrels, and loaded the weapon. Then he put the shotgun into the special sling sewn inside his jacket. He hoped like hell there would be no call to bring the devastating little weapon into use, especially against soldiers of his own country, but it felt good to have it there just in case.

Having no desire to make a long and arduous journey afoot with the Indian tribe, Faro had volunteered to ride with the braves who were herding the horses south. When the Indians reached their destination and turned the horses loose, he would continue on south while the braves started back north to rejoin their tribe. Only a few days of travel, he figured, would bring him to some road which he could take south toward San Francisco and the fortune in gold which he hoped was waiting for him there.

At the mouth of the cave Faro was about to follow the trail most of the others had already taken, but a most unusual activity going on to one side made him stop and stare in puzzlement. In a large iron pot over an open fire, Evening Star and her young helper were preparing a stew which looked and smelled very similar to the one the tribe had feasted on the night before. As he watched they dumped in a surprising amount of the tribe's precious food stores, including several bags of jerked deer meat and great handfuls of dried plants and vegetables.

Finally he was moved to ask, "What are you cooking now for? Nobody's going to have time to eat before they start out. Almost everybody's gone already."

Looking up from her work with a sly grin on her face, Evening Star announced, "The white soldiers might be hungry when they come here looking for us."

"What? You're leaving a pot of stew for them?" Faro asked.

"Yes, my brother," Evening Star said. "But it's a very special pot of stew which might buy us some extra time if they decide to try some of it." From a pack beside her, she took out a small leather bag and began sprinkling a whitish powder into the stewpot. Her helper quickly stirred it in.

Faro laughed out loud as he watched. If the soldiers got this far and did decide to try a taste of the apparently deserted meal, they would get a whole lot more out of it than they had bargained for. Volney's men might lose a whole day trying to return from never-never land before they took up the chase.

When the stew was complete and simmering nicely over the fire, Faro accompanied the priestess and her companion over to the edge of the lava beds. The afternoon sun had already disappeared below the horizon to the west, and the last light of day was quickly dissolving into night. Faro led the horse he chose to ride to the place where Ashford and Burning Wind were conferring over the route of their first night's march.

The two men rose from the improvised map the scout had drawn on the ground and turned to meet him.

"Well, I'd be a damned liar if I said I'd enjoyed this whole thing," Faro said, shaking both men's hands. "But I'll admit it has been different."

"We wish you well, my friend," Burning Wind told him solemnly.

"Yeah, you watch out for your backside now, Blake," Ashford advised. "I know you'll do all right. It's easy to tell you're one of those surviving kind of fellows."

"I wish the same to you," Faro told them. "But I can't say I envy you the road ahead. Even when you reach Canada, you know, your people can't go on living the same way they have been indefinitely. All this you've done, and all you're going to do, all it does is gain you a few more years."

"That's as much as anything gets anybody," Burning Wind told him philosophically.

Chapter Twelve

They made a fireless camp in a patch of woods on the south bank of the Mako River at least sixty miles south of their starting point at the lava beds. It had been an exhausting trip for Faro and the four Leather-foot braves who accompanied him driving the horses south. The first night they had traveled only about twenty miles, but the following day they gained forty more, finally reaching the bank of the river and crossing it with the herd shortly before dusk.

The animals were grazing peacefully now in a grassy meadow a few hundred yards away. Two of the braves had gone back north to see how close the pursuing troops were, and Faro and the other two pitched camp and settled down to their first complete night's rest in more than two days. Faro, at least, was looking forward to it with great relish.

The four Indians and Faro had decided that if the soldiers were far enough behind, then the five of them would drive the horses on southward for another day before abandoning them. But if the two braves who were out now returned with news that the soldiers were close by, then they would immediately scatter the herd and take off on foot in their separate directions. Either way, Faro figured, the ploy had probably brought the Leatherfeet time enough to get safely out of Volney's reach.

For supper that night they dined on jerked venison and a thick, pasty substance which the two Indians produced from their small packs of provisions. The gummy stuff seemed to be made of dried berries, ground vegetables, and some of the flour stolen from the fort's larders, but Faro didn't ask for specifics—it was filling and apparently nutritious, and that was all that mattered at this point. Steaks aplenty awaited him when he reached San Francisco.

It was completely dark when they finished eating and spread their blankets to rest. Faro shucked off his jacket, vest, and boots, then wandered off into the brush to relieve himself before lying down.

He was about twenty feet from camp, squatting with his trousers down around his ankles, when the commotion began. There were no shouts or loud noises, but the dull thumps and moans which he did hear were enough to tell him that something was mighty wrong somewhere nearby. When he had left camp the two Indians had both been flat on their backs, ready to fall asleep, and the noises he now heard did not jibe with that.

These things always happen when a man's just settled down to crap in the woods, Faro thought bitterly. A legendary deer comes within shooting range, a bear or a bobcat decides the opportunity is right to turn you into dinner . . . or some blamed fool picks that precise moment to attack your camp.

As he hurriedly finished and rose to his feet, he heard the sound of hushed voices through the bushes.

"Well, where is he? His blankets are here alongside these other two." It was a white man's voice, and Faro scoured his memory, trying to figure out why it sounded familiar.

"Maybe go poot. We wait for him here." The dialect of that one was clearly Indian, and even in a whispered tone, Faro recognized the voice as that of Woodpecker, the renegade Leatherfoot. It was a sure bet, he knew, that Jay Feather was close by, too.

As silence closed in around him Faro's first impulse was to plunge off into the brush, trusting the darkness and the twisting tangle of scrub to aid him in his escape. But as he stood for a moment, silently buttoning his trousers and buckling his belt, he felt a growing anger overtake him. Could he stand himself if he just ran cravenly away and let these bastards get away with this?

There were plenty of good reasons not to run. For one thing, his boots, clothing, weapons, and most especially every cent of his money, were still back at the camp. And even if he could suffer the loss of everything else, including his cash, he couldn't gain much speed or distance on his pursuers barefooted.

But besides all that, there was a personal sort of thing involved here, too. Jay Feather and Woodpecker were rotten sons of bitches, backshooting bastards who in the end had considered their own survival more important than the survival of their entire tribe. Faro was not the kind to crusade for worthy causes very often, but he did know it would give him a lot of private satisfaction to lay those two low. And whoever the white man was, if he was with these two then he was probably the same trashy sort.

Quickly Faro peeled out of his white shirt, realizing

what a visible target it would make him at night. Then he worked his way slowly and cautiously forward, knowing that his first step would be to determine where the three men were. Near the edge of camp he dropped to his hands and knees and silently crawled the last few feet. In the dim starlight, he could vaguely make out the details before him.

No more than a yard away lay the body of one of Faro's Indian companions, still stretched out on his blanket as he had been when Faro left. The second Leatherfoot lay on the far side of the first, twisted around awkwardly. There was no doubt in Faro's mind that both were now dead at the hands of their former tribesmen. Farther away the three attackers were crouched around on various sides of the twenty-foot clearing, waiting silently for him to return and fall into their trap.

Faro figured that the single idea he came up with was right close to the top of the list of the world's oldest tricks. Cavemen warriors had probably pitched stones on the opposite side of their enemies, hoping to distract them long enough to bash them in the head with their clubs.

But then, he decided, maybe the trick had stuck around so long because it still worked on tension-charged men who were waiting for a fight.

Hidden in the edge of the brush, Faro took at least a minute to rise silently to a crouch. Then he felt around on the ground nearby until he found a stone about the size of his fist. Timing would be essential now, and he knew he would have only an instant of confusion to make his play.

He hurled the rock with all his might at the shadowy figure straight across from him twenty feet away. As it landed with a satisfying thud the man's gun discharged with a sudden, startling roar. By that time, Faro was already in action.

He leaped forward and rolled across his dead companions to the place where he had laid his jacket, praying that the attackers had not moved it. He found the coat and fumbled momentarily with it, searching for the shotgun, just as a shot rang out no more than ten feet away. He heard the slug thump into the already dead Indian beside him.

He brought the gun up and fired it point-blank at the dark form charging toward him, then rolled to the side to avoid being buried by the man's falling body. At the same time he swung the shotgun around and discharged the second chamber at another man who was firing wildly into the tangle of bodies in the center of the clearing. The Indian cut loose with an earsplitting shriek, the last sound his mortal remains would ever issue. His mangled body spread-eagled into the brush behind him.

Another thick silence suddenly settled over the clearing, and Faro lay still for a moment, straining his ears for any noise or sign of movement around him. He wasn't really worried about the two Indians any longer —the sawed-off shotgun wasn't the sort of weapon that left a man only wounded, especially at these close quarters—but there had been a third man here, and Faro wasn't so sure about him.

Finally he grappled around until he found his coat and drew two more shotgun shells out of a pocket, then risked the necessary clicking noises to reload the weapon. Still there was no sign of movement around him. He rose to his feet, holding the shotgun in one hand like a pistol as he probed the darkness with it, and started toward where the third attacker had been earlier.

He found the man sprawled out on the ground and

quickly kicked his rifle away. Then by the light of a match Faro made certain that he was unconscious. The rock had apparently struck the man in the center of his forehead, but the splash of blood across his face was not enough to disguise his identity—it was Karl Dober, the sergeant who had been so intent on seeing how far Faro's neck would stretch that night at the Redwood Roundup Saloon.

After determining that Dober was still among the living, Faro grabbed him by the collar and dragged him roughly to the river. It took several dunkings to bring the sergeant back to life, but finally he emerged from the water sputtering and struggling. Faro dunked him one more time for good measure, holding his head under for half a minute, then raised him up and flung him aside on the bank of the river.

"Whaaa . . . whoooo . . . wass goin' on?" Dober said in between gags and coughs.

"I've just shipped your two friends off to their happy hunting grounds," Faro snarled at him, "and you're fixing to join them shortly—that is, if they let palefaced jackasses in there, too."

Dober opened his mouth to ask "Who are you?" but the words came out garbled as Faro thrust the twin barrels of his shotgun into the sergeant's mouth.

"Hell, you oughta recognize an old gambling buddy like me, Sarge," Faro taunted him. "After all, we damn near shared a span of rope together once—you on the pulling end and me on the swinging end. I'm Faro Blake."

Dober answered with a series of mmumaphs and gnarrakks which seemed to indicate that he knew he had some serious problems here.

"Now, when I take this gun out of your mouth," Faro continued, "I'm going to ask some questions, and I hope to hell you're in the proper frame of mind to answer them for me. Otherwise . . ." He swung the barrel of the shotgun to the side of Dober's head and discharged one barrel into the ground only inches away. The sergeant convulsed in terror beneath him.

"First question," Faro said. "How far away are Volney and his men?"

"Thirty, maybe forty miles," Dober croaked. His throat was constricted with fear and his voice was raspy and high-pitched. "Some of the troops ate out of a big stewpot near them Injun caves, figuring the redskins left in such a hurry that they didn't even bother to eat their dinner. It made the men crazy all night, and it was early this morning before they finally got in shape to ride."

"Well, then, what were you doing way out ahead like this, and in the company of them two skunks back there?"

"It was the horses. We were after the horses," Dober explained. "Woodpecker and Jay Feather was hiding in the rocks and saw the tribe split up. They figured out what the plan was and then come to get me. We was going to take the horses and keep heading on south with them till we come to some place safe to sell them at."

"So you didn't say anything to Volney about it?" Faro asked. "He doesn't know that the tribe really went north?"

"No. I deserted. Me and them two figured we could keep ahead of Volney and lose him somewhere in the mountains to the south."

"You stupid son of a bitch," Faro growled. "If you'd just trailed us for another day or so you could have had them horses free of charge, without having to kill anybody and without having to end up in the lousy predicament you're in now. But you didn't wait, and now it looks pretty bad for you, old boy."

"Don't kill me, Blake," the sergeant pleaded. "This could still work out the same way, but only with you and me taking them animals south instead of me an' them redskins. There'd be plenty of money to be made sellin' that herd to one of the ranches south of here."

"I've never had no fondness for horses," Faro admitted. "Probably the only thing I'd think worse of than a long horseback ride is making such a trip in the company of a belly-crawling, yellow-tailed skunk that couldn't be trusted not to slit his own mama's throat if the money was right. Nope, Dober. You ain't got yourself no new partner."

"Well, what are you going to do, then?" Dober asked. "You can't just kill me in cold blood!"

"I admit it wouldn't be the fair or Christian thing to do," Faro told him. "But if I remember right, you've already had me pegged for a crook, anyway. And as far as the other part goes, well, I'd rather live by the scripture that calls an eye for an eye than the one that says love your enemies."

Dober was quivering and limp with terror as Faro jerked him to his feet and started back toward the camp with him, but he was not too frightened to continue his pleas for his life.

"For God's sake, Blake!" he croaked. "I hadn't done nothing to you bad enough to be killed over. We didn't hang you that day in town, did we? And as far as this stuff out here went, well, you come out of it all right, didn't you? The onliest ones that didn't fare so well was them four Injuns, which ain't hardly no loss as I see it."

"Maybe you're right," Faro said as he kicked the sergeant's feet out from under him and slammed him to the ground with his back against a tree. "Maybe I ain't got no call to deal so harshly with you, after all." He located a length of rope from beside one of the dead

Leatherfeet, then tied Dober's hands behind him around the tree as he continued. "But, just to be fair, one of us ought to stay behind so when them other two Leatherfeet get back, there'll be somebody here in the camp to tell them what happened and how their friends ended up dead. I'm volunteering you for that job, Dober."

The sergeant's eyes grew huge with horror, but Faro silenced his pleas and protests by stuffing a wad of cloth into his mouth and securing it with Dober's own neckerchief. Then, with his hostage completely silenced and immobilized, he turned and began gathering up his clothing and gear. In a moment, he had his advantage tool case in one hand, his bedroll in the other, and was ready to leave.

"Now, when them two Indians get back here," Faro advised, "you just explain to them how the killing of their two friends don't hardly count for nothing because they was just two worthless redskins. It isn't like no white man was harmed in any way, is it, old son?"

With grunts and garbled moans, Dober tried to make a final plea, but it did no good.

"No, there ain't no need to thank me, Sarge," Faro said. "I know them two are going to give you just as much understanding as you merit. Yes, sir, I'd say you're going to get just what you deserve from them."

With that final pronouncement, Faro headed off through the brush toward where the herd was grazing.

Chapter Thirteen

Faro Blake sat in the dining room of the Carilinda House, a swank hotel on the edge of the Nob Hill district of San Francisco. Before him lay the remnants of the huge, uncustomary breakfast he had just finished, along with a brimming cup of coffee liberally laced with brandy from his pocket flask. He felt damned good.

It had taken him two full weeks to work his way down from the Leatherfoot country to the City by the Bay, traveling as inconspicuously as possible because of the chance that Major Volney might have sent word out about him and Ashford. He had used an assumed name and had stopped in only the smallest communities and towns for supplies along the way. But, despite his precautions, he had not heard one thread of talk about the army looking for a gambler named Faro Blake nor a scout named Jason Ashford. Faro could only assume that Volney was not searching for them to the south because he believed they had fled north with Burning Wind and his band. By the time he reached San Francisco, Faro discarded his fake handle and checked in at the Carilinda House under his real name.

He tipped the cup to his lips and savored the rich flavor of the coffee, then drew a long, slim cigar from his pocket, snipped the ends, and lit up. Tramping around the wilderness, he reflected, fighting for the rights of the downtrodden and crusading for noble causes might be all right sometimes. Hell, every man probably ought to experience a little bit of that once in a while. But there was definitely something to be said for the creature comforts of city life, too, decadent though they sometimes were. A man just had to set his priorities.

When he saw a newsboy threading his way through the tables of the restaurant, Faro waved him over and bought a paper. It would be good, he thought, to read some news that was less than half a month old, and there might be something about how things were going out at the Estrella del Norte.

The front page held no articles of interest to him, but as he turned to the inside an article on page three immediately drew his attention. The headline read:

Fort Commander Faces
Court-Martial Board

The article explained how Major Nehemiah Volney, commander of a small outpost in the northern part of the state, had been recalled to army headquarters at Monterey to face court-martial proceedings for his mishandling of the recent Leatherfoot Indian crises. The charges against him ranged from taking improper precautions to secure his station while he was away to general incompetence and disregard for the safety and welfare of his men.

In his own defense, the article said, Volney blamed all his failures on the desertion of his scout, Jason Ashford, who had apparently gone over to the Indian side and helped the Leatherfeet deceive the army and make their escape. At present, it went on to relate, the whereabouts of the entire Leatherfoot tribe was still a mystery.

Grinning broadly, Faro laid the paper aside and gulped down the entire contents of his cup. Then he refilled it with brandy from the flask and shot that back, too. There had been no mention of his name at all in the article. Apparently Volney considered his part in the whole affair so inconsequential as to not even rate a mention, which suited Faro fine.

In a few moments he paid the bill for his meal and left the restaurant, starting down the street toward a nearby print shop. The day before, his first in San Francisco, he had been mulling over every detail of a plan to get back in with Amos Harbison and claim a share of the Estrella del Norte mine. Now he was ready to set everything in motion.

He had his story worked out about why he had been gone so long and had finally reappeared without the machinery he had set out to buy. On his way overland to Denver, where the drilling machine was to be bought, he had been accosted by robbers in the badlands of Utah, and they had taken every cent of the five thousand dollars Harbison had advanced him. But later, Faro would explain, he had set out after the robbers, mercilessly tracking them down and killing them one by one, until at last they were all dead and he had regained the entire five thousand.

Handing the money back over to Harbison, he decided, would be a nice touch. Hell, what was the sacrifice of five thousand dollars compared to the fifty percent profits he would soon be raking in?

The business about the engineering report which Harbison demanded as proof of Simon Carmody's identity did bother Faro some, but he could just explain that it had been destroyed by the bandits. He could kick himself for having burned it in the first place, but that was the way things were and he would just have to live with it.

A bell on the door announced his arrival in the print shop, and in a moment a man wearing an ink-smeared apron met him at the counter.

"Yessir," the man said. "What can I do for you?"

"I've just arrived back in town and I need some calling cards made," Faro told him. "The name's Simon Carmody."

In an instant the man's smile turned into a leering grin and he reached under the counter before him. "There should be no problem with that, sir," he announced. He produced a large sheet of paper with several samples of calling cards glued on it. Faro's jaw dropped as he looked down and saw that every card on the paper bore the same name—Simon Carmody.

"I've had such a run on these since that piece came out in the paper about the Estrella del Norte that I finally just made up a sample sheet," the printer said with a chuckle. He pointed to the top card on the paper and said, "Now, here's a classy little number, the English Script, but I'll have to admit most of the more serious and businesslike gents have been going for this second one here, the Bodoni Bold. Now, this style down here, the Cater Script . . ."

"Forget it," Faro told him, turning away toward the door in disgust. Maybe, he thought, Harbison might get drunk enough to recognize him again if he went up and hung around the Pacific Palace for a few days in a row. And maybe not. Either way, he wouldn't hold his breath until it happened.